Expiry Dating

Bluestone Series: Book Two

Isobel Reed

Love Tools: Bluestone Series: Book Two
Copyright © 2022 Isobel Reed
All rights reserved.

ISBN: (print) 978-1-958136-35-5
(ebook) 978-1-958136-34-8

Inkspell Publishing
207 Moonglow Circle #101
Murrells Inlet, SC 29576

Cover art by: Fantasia Frog Designs
Edited by: Yezanira Venecia

DEDICATION

For the Ali in my life, love you.

ISOBEL REED

CHAPTER ONE

Alice stared down at her phone in horror.

"No, no, no. This cannot be happening. Goddamn lying, cheating, son of a bitch."

Her phone was never going to survive this. A loud thud echoed around the room after it went flying through the air and crashed against the dark wood walls of her cabin. Truthfully, as soon as she clicked on the picture, her cell phone never had a chance.

It had been three months since she'd caught her ex-boyfriend in bed with her best friend, two months since she had quit her job, and one month since she'd begged her sister, Lily, to let her come stay with her on her ranch in Bluestone County. Alice had enough self-awareness to admit she was running away from her problems, but being in London right now wasn't an option. And after just seeing her ex-best friend's latest social media post, it was a good thing Alice was in another country, otherwise there was a strong possibility she would've been locked up for grievous bodily harm by now.

"Oh my God, Ali, what the hell did you do to your phone? The screen is all cracked!" Lily gasped.

Alice hadn't even heard Lily come in. She was checking

on her again; she'd been doing that a lot.

"Um … yeah, it fell. Don't worry, I'm sure I can get it fixed in town."

Lily's jade eyes narrowed. "Oh, really? And where exactly did it fall from, Ali? The sky? 'Cos from where I'm standing, it looks like it either magically fell from the ceiling, or you threw it across the room in a fit of rage?"

This is the problem with being so close to your sister. She knows me too damn well.

Letting out a sigh, Alice slumped further down into the leather armchair that had been cocooning her for the past hour.

"Fucking Becky." She grumbled. "Apparently, she's pregnant. I'll give you three guesses as to who the father is."

And there it was, pity, all over her big sister's face.

"Oh, Ali. I'm so sorry. How did you find out?"

"My friend forwarded me a post Becky made."

Lily closed the distance between them and took a hold of Alice's hand, quickly pulling her up from the chair. "Come on. Let's go up to the main house. We can drink some wine, eat a fuckload of chocolate, and plot revenge."

Alice reluctantly followed. Wine and chocolate were probably the only things that could possibly salvage today.

They were just a two-minute walk from the main house where Lily and her husband, Jake, lived. Jake's sister, Sam, used to live there too but had recently moved in with her boyfriend, Duke.

Lily had initially wanted Alice to stay in the house with them, but she wanted the newlyweds to have some privacy. After all, it had only been two weeks since they'd gotten hitched in Vegas. Not to mention, Alice needed her own space. Luckily, the ranch had guest cabins, so she was able to take up residence in one of them until she figured out her next move.

As they walked into the house and made their way into the spotless stainless-steel kitchen, a familiar voice pricked up the hair on the back of her neck.

No. Please don't be here right now. Please, not today of all days.

Damnit. There he was—Brady—all six foot two of him. The new bane of her existence. He was wearing a fitted, tan, cop uniform so sexy it should be illegal. If she didn't already know he was the devil, she could easily be fooled by his dark, brooding good looks. Even his damn caramel-coloured eyes were mesmerizing.

Mesmerizing eyes? Get a frigging grip, Alice. He's the devil, remember?

It had been two weeks since they'd met in Vegas at Lily and Jake's impromptu wedding, and despite trying to avoid Brady like the plague since then, he just kept showing up. Yes, Bluestone was small, and Alice was staying at his best friend's ranch, but it was actually getting ridiculous. He was everywhere. Whenever she ventured out, whether it was to get coffee or go shopping, he was there, waiting in the shadows, ready to make her life miserable.

"Looking good, sweetness." Brady smirked as he purposely knocked her on the way over to the fridge, where he swiftly removed a beer bottle.

Alice shot him a glare over her shoulder. "Wish I could say the same to you, Brady, but it appears as if the rumours really are true and beer does go straight to a man's gut."

She was lying, of course. There was no beer belly in sight. The man was a wall of solid muscle, but something about him drove her absolutely insane. It apparently also meant she couldn't control her mouth whenever he was in the vicinity. He'd somehow managed to crawl under her skin in a matter of minutes of them meeting, and insults had been hurled between them ever since.

Brady's silky laughter bellowed behind her. "You offering to help me work it off, sweetness?"

She turned around just in time to catch his wink and saw red.

"For the love of God, stop calling me sweetness."

Storming over to the fridge, she pushed him out of the way, reached for the white wine, and waved it at him. "You want me to beat you with the bottle? Maybe you could burn off a few calories trying to fend me off?"

"Jesus. Will you two cut it out?" Jake's voice boomed across the kitchen.

She forgot they had an audience. The last thing she wanted to do was piss off her new brother-in-law, who right now looked every bit the cowboy; he was donned in his muddy jeans, flannel shirt, and black Stetson. Lily was currently enveloped in his arms, trying her very best to stifle a snigger. At least she wasn't mad. That was something.

"Hey, I'm trying to play nice, man"—Brady held up his hands in mercy—"but this chick is something else."

"Chick? Really?" Alice scolded.

"Yeah, sweetness, *chick*. Go ahead, tell me all the reasons why you're insulted by that term. I know you want to."

What she wouldn't do to wipe that smug grin off his way-too-handsome face. *Bastard.*

"Try not to choke on your beer, Brady—you've managed to piss off the only one of us here who knows CPR."

"Oh, sweetness, we both know you're dying to give me mouth-to-mouth." As if it were possible, Brady's smile got even wider, which only infuriated her more.

After very maturely flipping him off, she took her bottle and retreated into the living room, ignoring his laughter.

Even before her behind hit the couch, she could hear Lily and Jake plotting. They were doing it again: working out how to separate Alice and Brady before another argument ensued.

A moment later, Lily bounced down next to Alice and shot her a look. The look that only her big sister could give her. The "I'm disappointed in you, Alice" look.

"Why didn't you tell me Deputy Douche was gonna be here?" Alice asked.

"Really? We're gonna have this conversation again, Ali?"

Alice made quick work of opening the wine bottle and taking a healthy gulp before offering it to Lily. She shook her head at the offer and continued her rant. "What the hell is up with you two? I've never seen you like this with anyone before!"

Alice snorted at that. "Yeah, well, I hadn't had the pleasure of meeting dickwad out there before now."

"Uh-huh. Well, maybe you should try and tamper down all that charm of yours. He's a cop, y'know? He knows where to hide the bodies."

Alice knew where this conversation headed. It wasn't the first time she had heard it. In fact, her sister had given her the talk at least three times already over the past two weeks. Brady was Jake's best friend, and he wasn't going anywhere. And seeing as Alice wasn't going anywhere anytime soon, Lily wanted them to at least try to get along. But it wasn't that easy. Alice had tried to ignore him, avoided engaging with him, and what did the jerk do? He poked her. Poked and poked and poked until she couldn't stand it any longer and told him where to go. It was almost as if the sicko took pleasure in sparring with her.

She took another swig of wine and winced at the sharp tang lingering on her tongue.

He's literally driving me to drink.

"Maybe you should be having this conversation with him, Lilypad? It takes two to tango and all that."

"What do you think Jake is doing right now?"

"Well, then, great. I can't wait to meet the new and improved Deputy Douche."

ISOBEL REED

CHAPTER TWO

"As I live and breathe, Alice Hart, fancy running into you here." It had only been a day since Brady had last ruffled Alice's feathers, yet he could hardly wait to go another round.

He couldn't help but grin as he watched her curse a blue streak under her breath. He was a bastard. He knew it. She knew it. But for some reason, he just couldn't help himself. She brought out a side of him he never even knew he had. For once, he didn't feel numb.

"Do I need to get a restraining order? Stop bloody following me, will you!"

Brady calmly greeted a startled George with a nod, who, by the looks of it, was examining Alice's cracked phone screen.

Ignoring her outburst, Brady continued. "Let me guess. You cracked your screen by assaulting another unsuspecting victim with it?"

Before she could lay into him, George cleared his throat to get her attention, then declared, "I'll have to replace the whole screen. Give me a day and you can come by and pick it up tomorrow."

After waiting for her to thank George, Brady quietly

followed her out of the store. She didn't look back. Actually, she tried her damned hardest to pretend that he wasn't there.

For a moment, he thought twice about following her. But as his gaze returned to the sassy brunette, in her pretty little sundress, he couldn't resist.

Do her hips sway even more when she's mad? Shit. Focus.

Easily catching up, he took his place walking alongside her on the cobbled sidewalk. "Something up, sweetness?"

Silence. She was definitely ignoring him.

"How 'bout you let me turn that frown upside down?" he tried again.

Nothing. Not even a glare.

"Come on, darlin', you really gonna give me the silent treatment?"

Alice came to a halt and turned her flaming blue eyes at him. That was more like it. There was the fire he was looking for.

"What do you want, Brady?" Her voice was surprisingly composed, given the sparks of hostility shooting off her.

"Just being friendly, sweetness."

He watched her attempt to cool down by taking long, deep breaths, as if she was trying to suppress the urge to throat-punch him. Despite the obvious danger, he couldn't bring himself to walk away. Being in Alice Hart's company made him feel alive. As sad as it was, trading barbs with her was the best part of his day.

Yeah, that's healthy.

"Aren't you supposed to be being nice to me?" Alice's hands went to her hips as she waited for a response.

"Come again?" Brady's head tilted to the side as he let his eyes roam over her.

"You didn't get the talk the other day from Jake? The 'you need to try to get along' talk?"

Brady could feel his lips twitch. So that's what she was doing, attempting to avoid conflict with him. He'd endured at least three of those conversations from his best friend already. Something told him this wasn't the first one she'd received from her sister either. The real question was why Alice was choosing to listen now? Though if that's what she wanted, he was more than happy to play nice.

"When have I ever not been nice to you, sweetness? How 'bout I prove it by buying you a cup of coffee? Come on, let's go to Beano's."

She looked somewhat mortified by his suggestion, but he wasn't going to dwell on that. Before she could protest, he placed his hand on the small of her back and nudged her forward toward the café. They barely made it a few steps before Alice being Alice, came to a standstill.

"Stop. Just stop." He quickly dodged her flailing arms. "I don't want to have coffee with you, Brady. In fact, I would rather bathe in scolding hot coffee than share one with you."

"Now who's not being nice?"

A ridiculously cute growl escaped her lips while she stomped her foot onto the ground. Actually stomped. After that, he just couldn't help himself. He tried, he really did, but he couldn't halt the laugh that was soon making his whole body vibrate.

"Are you about done laughing at me?"

"Sorry, darlin', you're just so damn cute when you're angry."

She opened and closed her mouth a few times before she finally decided on her parting words. "Go to hell, Brady."

This time he didn't follow. He simply admired the view. *Yeah. I'm going to hell all right.*

***

Just a week after Brady had convinced himself he was going to hell, he finally made it there. The VA Clinic. There wasn't much fire and brimstone, but there was certainly a whole lot of dread.

Pocketing the keys to his truck, he reluctantly made his

way toward the building. It was one of those ultra-modern new buildings. Soulless. Bleak. And pretty hell-like.

Excellent.

He'd skipped his physio appointments for the past month and would have continued to happily skip them if his new boss hadn't threatened him with desk duty.

After checking in with the receptionist, Brady took a seat in the waiting room where he was assaulted by a homage to beige and brown. It was almost as if they wanted the place to look just as depressing as he felt.

Yeah, that's why you don't like coming here: you're offended by the décor.

He used the time to try and compartmentalize his thoughts. It had been almost seven months since he'd woken up in a hospital bed only to be handed his discharge papers. But being here, surrounded by other veterans, his resentment was starting to bubble to the surface again. New career or not, a marine was who he was. Who he'd always be.

Get your shit together, man.

"You've got to be kidding me."

As his eyes took in the sight of those familiar hips swaying toward him, Brady realised that getting his shit together wasn't going to be so simple. Not with his nerve endings now pulsating.

What the hell is she doing here?

As Alice came to a standstill before him, he took in the view from head to toe. It was good to know her signature frown was firmly in place. What wasn't firmly in place, though, was one of her many flowery dresses. No, she was dressed in workout clothes, and not just any workout clothes. Yoga pants, to be exact, that clung to every perfectly sculpted curve, so perfect that he thought he might choke on his tongue. It wasn't just the pants causing his mouth to dry up, though. The cropped tank top showcasing the silky, smooth bare skin across her midriff was doing a pretty good job of that too.

"Brady …? Brady …? Hello?"

A hard shove of his shoulder snapped him back to reality.

"Shit, sorry. What are you doing here, Ali?"

Alice tilted her head and quietly studied him. "I'm your new physical therapist. Why didn't I know you were doing PT?"

She's my what?!

"Like hell you are." Brady shot out of his seat, ready to educate the receptionist on all the reasons why Alice Hart would not be his new physical therapist.

Before he could even take his first stride, a soft hand on his chest sent a zing of electricity so strong it coursed through his whole body. It was so powerful, it had him freezing in his tracks.

"Brady. Why don't we go in the back and talk about this?" Her tone was almost soothing. He'd never witnessed her so calm. It was her eyes, though, that convinced him to follow her. Those deep blue pools were gentle and not helping with his now very urgent need for water.

A silent nod and a short walk from reception later, he found himself in her therapy room. He didn't immediately sit. He planned on getting some answers first.

"So … are you gonna tell me why I never knew you were a physical therapist?"

She was sitting at her desk, staring at a computer screen, likely reading his notes. Or re-reading them. "Probably the same reason I didn't know you were in need of physical therapy until today."

He couldn't do this. Not with her. As he reached for the door handle, he felt her head whip his way. "Don't." Just one word. Yet it was enough to make him think twice while she stood and closed the distance between them. When she got to him, she placed herself between him and the door.

"Look. I know we aren't exactly besties, but right now none of that matters. While I'm in this clinic, I'm a PT and nothing else, not Ali, not the chick who threatened to kick you in the balls, just a PT. And I'm a good one, so why don't you let me do my job? Let me help you."

Let me help you. Why does that sting so much?

"As nice as it is to know that my balls are in the forefront of your mind, sweetness, you still haven't answered my question. Why is it I didn't know you were a PT—a PT at the VA Clinic at that?"

He watched her professional mask momentarily falter.

"In case you hadn't noticed, Brady, we're not exactly friends. There would be no reason for you to know what I did for a living. As for the VA Clinic, this job is fairly new."

He knew they weren't friends, so why did his stomach twist with that little reality check?

"How new?"

"Today is my first day. Now, are you gonna let me do my job?"

"No." He reached around her to grasp the handle again, thinking she would take the hint and move. She didn't. Why was he not surprised? Instead, she moved toward him, essentially making herself a human barricade.

"Sweetness," he warned.

"Why are you doing this? Is it because you don't like me—is that it? Because I'm a professional, Brady; I can put aside our differences when I'm in this room."

Having her this close was not wise, let alone having her touch him. *Why does she smell like chocolate?*

"I think the real question here, darlin', is why are you so determined to be my PT?"

Something changed, her shoulders slumped and her features softened.

"I can't … it's my first day. I have a probationary period. If a client on my first day wants to be transferred—how is that gonna look?"

It was hard not to notice the silent pleading glistening in those sapphire eyes. Seeing this side of her was new. Vulnerable. She'd never once dropped her guard in his presence. It almost made him want to stay. Endure the humiliation, so he could see more of her like this. Just Ali.

Yeah, and let her see who you really are, who you've been hiding? A weak and broken loser. Then what will she think of you?

Then her hand went to his chest again. An innocent touch that shouldn't heat his blood or make him feel like his heart might pound right out of his chest. "Please, Brady."

Fuck.

Only ten minutes into his session and Brady was already regretting his decision to stay.

"And hold it there."

He saw the sadness in her eyes again as she added more pressure to his leg.

He should have avoided eye contact. He should have plucked her delicate fingers off his shirt and never looked back, because then he wouldn't be here right now. In the seventh circle of hell. No, he'd be enjoying his lunchtime dose of caffeine. Instead, he was here with Alice Hart, allowing her to torture him. If he didn't die from these damn exercises, then he'd burn from the heat engulfing his whole body every time she touched him.

"What's that face for? Am I hurting you?" Alice's voice cut through his chain of thought.

Yes. "No, I'm fine. Are we done yet?"

"Seriously, Brady, I need to know your limits. If I'm going to be able to help you, you need to tell me what you're feeling."

He couldn't take it anymore. The pain radiating from his knee, the look of pity on her face, her soft hands on his body. It was all too much.

"You wanna know what I'm feeling, Ali? Really?" Anger started to boil. "I *feel* that I'm about sick and tired of you giving me those goddamn pitiful looks and talking to me like I'm made of fucking glass."

Pushing aside the pain, he brought himself up and off the mat.

Any pity he thought he'd seen on Alice's face had quickly been replaced with anger. "That's what this is about … your precious male ego?"

He ignored her motion to scramble up and made a beeline for the door.

"Don't you dare walk out that door, Brady Mitchell," she roared after him.

But it was too late. He'd tried. He really had.

CHAPTER THREE

Perched on the bar stool at Mickey's, Alice took another sip of her celebratory gin and tonic. Sure, her new job was temporary, but it felt good to be doing what she loved again. She had finished her first week at the VA Clinic, and with the exception of Brady showing up on her first day, it had gone well.

Brady Mitchell. There he was clouding her thoughts again. Why did he have to be so pig-headed?

Because he's an arsehole.

Yes, he was. And she needed to remember that. In fact, she needed to repeat the words *pig-headed arsehole* over and over again in her head the next time she dared touch him.

Her head was in charge now. Especially now she knew her body was clearly full of crap and couldn't be trusted. It had no business making any kind of decisions on her behalf. Not after Rob. No, she could not and would not let another man have any kind of power over her ever, ever again.

Bring on the cats.

"Mind if I join you?" A husky voice jolted her out of her thoughts.

She looked up, surprised to find Ryan, the chef at Jake and Lily's ranch. Decent-looking guy. He had the whole tall, dark, and handsome thing going on. From what she could tell, he seemed nice enough. Not that she was a great judge of character or anything.

"Hey, sure, take a seat. I'm celebrating."

One corner of his mouth picked up. "Is that so? By yourself?"

"Yep. Me, myself, and I."

That lopsided smile slowly turned into a fully-fledged grin, and she didn't quite know what to make of it. She didn't know Ryan that well, but she had a strong feeling that a grin like the one currently aimed her way would bring a lot of women to their knees. Maybe even literally.

"Well, I guess I better get you another." He gestured to the bartender, Teddy, and pointed at her drink. A very male, silent communication passed between them and ended with another drink being placed in front of her. "What are we celebrating?"

Oh, what the hell. I deserve it.

Two drinks later and she was pleased to learn that Ryan was indeed a nice guy. She'd shared with him details of her new job and in turn he'd talked about how he became a chef. The man was a shameless flirt, of course, but she seemed to be pretty immune to his charms. It made her wonder if maybe she was broken. Had Rob broken her?

It had been over three months since her break-up and she hadn't so much as looked twice at another man. Well, actually, that wasn't quite true. There was one man she'd looked at more than twice, but that was never going to happen. But the point was, here she was, sharing a drink with an attractive man, who pre-Rob would have been just her type, and she felt nothing. Zero. Zilch. Nada.

Yep, I'm definitely broken.

Suddenly in need of a bathroom break, she excused herself and went in pursuit of the ladies' room. She felt him before she saw him. Brady, leaning against the aging crimson wallpaper, his very angry eyes on her.

Fuckity fuck.

She hadn't seen him since he'd stormed out on her,

which was unusual, considering he had a habit of just showing up wherever she was. Despite him being a pig-headed arsehole, she knew she had to talk to him at some point and convince him to show up to his next session. But now was not the time. She was two drinks in, and he was looking at her like she'd just slapped his mum and shot his dog.

Adjusting her path so she didn't have to pass him, Alice thought she could avoid the looming confrontation. She was wrong. Before she reached the door to the ladies', a strong arm was on hers, swivelling her around to face him. Already in her space, he kept inching forward until her back hit the wall. That's when he crowded her, one hand resting next to her face.

"Ever heard of personal space?" The words came out a little more breathless than she'd hoped. Having Brady this close to her was not good. Not good at all. He even smelled sexy.

Pig-headed arsehole, remember?

"Sure have, sweetness. You wanna tell me what you're doing here with Ryan?"

"What?"

"You on a date?"

Is he jealous? No, he couldn't be; he hates me.

"That's none of your business."

Brady's eyes narrowed—they were the darkest she'd ever seen them. "Like hell it's not. You think I'm gonna sit back and let you shack up with the town whore?"

"*Let me?*" she spat. "I don't know what your dysfunction is, Brady, but the last time I checked, you have no control whatsoever of who I talk to, date, or *fuck*."

His expression turned granite as his breath hit her skin and the notes of whiskey on his breath filled her nostrils. "You're playing with fire, darlin'."

"Is that so? And what exactly are you gonna do?"

Quicker than lightning, she was airborne and over his shoulder, her arse in the air. He was carrying her out of the bar like a Neanderthal, but she didn't go quietly. She treated the bar to a show, mostly of her punching his back and shouting that he put her down. He didn't even flinch.

It wasn't until they reached his truck that he let her down, but it wasn't on her feet. No, Brady placed her inside his truck and began buckling her in, calmly. Like he hadn't just tossed her over his shoulder and carried her out against her will.

Jesus Christ. The man is unhinged. Batshit fucking crazy.

She released the seatbelt as soon as she could and attempted to barge her way out. She didn't get very far. Actually, she was still in the truck seat, sans seatbelt.

Damn wall of muscle.

"I'll call the police, Brady. I mean it."

His smile made an appearance then, and she knew she wasn't going to like what he said next.

"I am the police, sweetness, remember?"

"I think they call that abuse of power. Just 'cos you're a cop, doesn't mean you can go around kidnapping people 'cos you think you can get away with it."

"Sweetness, I'm not gonna stand 'round here arguing with you. I'm taking you home. You've been drinking, you can't drive, and I'm sure as hell not gonna leave you with Ryan."

"I've had two drinks, Brady. You're being ridiculous."

He didn't answer this time, he just reached for the belt buckle and tried again. She let out a frustrated groan. This man was going to be the death of her.

As she settled back in the seat, she prayed the gin would kick in soon. Tonight was supposed to be about celebrating a new life and, instead, she was back to feeling broken. She didn't fight this time; there wasn't much left in her. Not tonight anyway.

The car journey was silent. Not even one snarky comment left either of their lips. But that wasn't the strangest part. The real shocker was that now Brady was in her cabin.

Why was he in her cabin? She didn't have a damn clue. After they had arrived at the ranch, he walked down with her and just sort of invited himself inside. It was all very odd, but it didn't change the fact that he was there. In her space. Somehow making her small home feel even smaller than it was.

"Um ... do you want a drink?"

What the hell am I saying? I should kick him out, yell at him, call him a caveman.

"Please." His tone was soft. He was never soft. *What on earth is going on?*

He followed her into the shabby chic kitchenette and sat down at her tiny table. As she sneaked a glance over at him, she had to bite back a laugh. His legs were too long to even go under the table, and he had to position them to one side. He was so damn big. It was almost comical.

Swallowing her silly thoughts, she reached into the fridge and grabbed two bottles of water before taking the seat across from him. The smile she received was disarming, which was probably why she decided that now was as good a time as any to talk about his physical therapy.

"We should talk about what happened the other day ..."

"No." Gone was the smile, replaced with the familiar knit in his brow.

Alice let out a heavy sigh. "You can't just dismiss me like that, Brady. I know you hate me. I know you think I'm a bitch—"

"I don't hate you, Ali, and I definitely don't think you're a bitch."

That surprised her. "You don't?" She didn't want to analyse why that caused a pang in her chest. "But, I-I thought that ... i-i-it's just that ..."

Great. Now I'm stuttering.

"What happened at the clinic. It wasn't about you. It was about me. I think ... I want you to transfer me to someone else."

"No."

"No?" he repeated.

"No. I'm not gonna transfer you to someone else. On Monday, we will pick up where we left off."

He ran his hands through his dark hair. "I don't think you understand what I'm saying. Ali. This is not optional. If you don't transfer me, then I just won't show."

Alice was trying her hardest to remain calm. She knew why he didn't want her working on him now. If it wasn't because he disliked her, then it could only be one other thing. He didn't want her to see him differently, which made sense, seeing as they were sparring partners and all.

"Then I will come to you. I will hunt you down, Brady Mitchell." The absurdity in her announcement seemed to disperse the lingering tension in the air. And just like that, Brady's lips curved up again.

"Oh, yeah? And what are ya gonna do when you find me, sweetness? Tie me to a chair and try and stretch my leg?"

Why did the thought of him tied to a chair bring a smile to her face?

"Maybe I will. But the fact remains, I'm not going anywhere. You're stuck with me. If that means spending the next few months hunting you down, then so be it."

The bastard just smirked at her for a full minute, a devilish glint in his chocolate eyes. "Well then, sweetness, I look forward to the chase."

And with that parting comment, he left her little cabin and didn't look back.

***

Alice watched on from the kitchen stool as her sister mixed flour and eggs in a large bowl. Lily had never been what one would call domesticated. When they were growing up, she could barely make toast let alone cakes. So this side of her, this new rancher's wife side of her, well, Alice didn't know what to make of that.

"When did you learn to bake again?" Alice asked, her eyes still transfixed on the whisk.

"Don't give me that look, Ali!"

She feigned innocence. "What look?"

"You know what look. I'm not doing this to please Jake. I'm doing this 'cos I like cake. End of story. So spare me your lecture."

Lily was clearly prickly, which made Alice wonder why. As far as she could see, her sister had it all: a beautiful place to live, a husband who adored her, and a successful business. Why would she even care what Alice thought?

Lily pushed a golden strand of hair out of her face before continuing. "Mum called again earlier. You know that every time you dodge her calls, she calls me instead?"

Alice did know that. And it made her feel bad, but not bad enough to return her mother's calls.

"You of all people should know what she's like, Lilypad. Remember when you first moved here? All the calls you got from her ... all the guilt trips?"

"Oh, I remember," her sister conceded, "but that doesn't mean you can just avoid her forever."

"It's not like I don't answer all of her calls. I answer *some* of them." Enough of them to wish she'd hit the reject button instead of answering.

"Well, answer some more." Lily gave her a pointed look.

Alice purposely didn't answer. She wasn't going to be making promises she had no intention of keeping.

"Anyway"—her sister moved on surprisingly quickly— "you gonna tell me what happened at Mickey's the other night?"

Of course her sister knew about Brady hauling her out of the bar. You couldn't hide a needle in a haystack in this tiny town.

"Nothing to tell, sis. Deputy Douche was being his charming self, as usual, only this time we had an audience."

"Hmm. That's not exactly what I heard."

"And what exactly *did* you hear, Lilypad?" Alice tried to

remain nonchalant, but she was curious to hear the gossip mill's take on it. Because she sure as hell was more than a little confused by it all.

"I heard that you and Brady were going at it and he manhandled you out of the bar."

Well, that was anti-climactic. "Yep, sounds about right."

"You know what I think?" *Here we go.* "I think … you guys like each other, and that's why you guys fight so much."

Alice's eyes rolled so hard they practically hit the back of her head. "Yes, because Brady and I scream *couple goals*."

Lily ignored Alice's sarcastic retort and carefully poured her concoction into cake tins before placing them into the oven. She then proceeded to wipe down the surface and wash her hands. The silence was deafening, and it only meant one thing. She was gearing up for her very own lecture. A lecture Alice did not have any intention of listening to.

"Okay, sis." Alice quickly rose and slapped her hands on the steel countertop. "Nice hanging out—"

"Oh, no you don't." Lily had walked around the counter and was now blocking Alice's retreat. "You are gonna sit, and you're gonna listen to what I have to say. Then, if you're nice to me, I'll let you have some of my cake."

Alice sat back on the stool and let out a huff. It wasn't like she could avoid her sister forever; she lived on Lily's property after all.

Taking a seat next to her, Lily launched right in. "I know you don't want to talk about Rob. I know it's painful. But by not talking about it, it's somehow making it worse. I've been patient with you; I haven't pushed. You needed time, and I wanted to give that to you … but enough. It's time."

Alice shifted in her chair, suddenly more uncomfortable than she'd ever felt. She wasn't ready to do this. It still felt too fresh.

Ignoring her clear discomfort, her sister continued. "Rob hurt you. He's a world-class shithead and Becky was always a jealous little cow, but now it's time to forget about them. It's time to heal. Maybe even put yourself out there again?"

Alice swallowed down the emotion clogging her throat. Yes, Rob had moved on. Well, really, he had moved on while still in a relationship with her, but that didn't mean she could. How was she supposed to trust anyone ever again? No, a relationship wasn't in her future. She could never give whatever was left of her heart to anyone ever again. It was already tattered; she needed to protect what was left.

"I'm not interested in getting back out there. I'm done. I've committed to a long and happy life with my vibrator."

Lily didn't even crack a smile. "So that's it? You're turning celibate at the grand old age of twenty-seven? You can't honestly tell me you have no plans to have sex ever again because that fuckwad hurt you?"

"Fine. I'm sure I'll shag someone in the next fifty years or so, but that's all it will be ever. I'm done with relationships. Everything will have an expiry date from now on." She snapped her fingers together. "It will be *expiry dating* from here on out."

ISOBEL REED

CHAPTER FOUR

Brady was hiding. Like a coward. He had missed his physical therapy appointment today, like he already said he would. It wasn't the thought of Alice Hart being on a rampage that had him cowering, because if anything, he lived for the blue fire in her eyes. No, he was hiding because it was easier than having to explain why he didn't want her to be his PT.

Being home or at the station was too obvious, so instead he chose to hide in plain sight. He was just finishing off his burger at the diner when she found him. And she looked pissed. Really pissed.

The red leather squeaked against her bare thighs as she slid into the booth seat across from him. She'd changed into one of her dresses, this one more form-fitting than the ones he was used to seeing her in.

Damn, she looks good.

She wasn't talking, so he took his time letting his eyes roam over her. Her long, dark waves were loose; he loved it when she wore her hair down. He wondered how it would feel in his fingers. Would it be as silky as it looked? The low-cut, strappy dress meant he was treated to miles of creamy skin, and all he could think about was how it might taste.

His tongue even darted out to lick his bottom lip. Apparently his body was on board with the idea too.

Stay strong, man. Don't cave, 'cause she's hot.

His gaze flicked back up to her face then, her death stare was still going strong, but she was yet to speak.

"Sweetness," he greeted, "something you wanna talk to me about?"

"Don't play dumb, Brady. You know why I'm here."

"To have dinner with me?"

"Cute." She waved down Dotty, the diner's owner, and requested the check before returning her glare back to him. "Seeing as you skipped out on your appointment today, I've decided to take matters into my own hands."

One brow involuntarily arched at her. "Is that so?"

Dotty placed the check on the table just as Alice was about to reply. After taking a quick glance, he pulled out a twenty and threw it on top of the bill.

"Ready?" Alice asked, sliding back out of the booth and looking at him expectantly.

What is her game?

She was being far too calm for his liking. Which meant she had a plan. A plan he no doubt wouldn't like.

Outside the diner, she let him lead the way and quietly followed him to his truck. He was not playing her game. He was going to get in his damn truck and drive home. Which was exactly what he started to do, that was until Alice appeared next to him in the passenger seat.

"What are you doing?" His tone took on a more serious note.

"I'm sitting in your car, Brady, what does it look like I'm doing?"

"Don't be a smartass. You trying to hitch a lift or something?"

She gave him those big puppy dog eyes that she thought made her look innocent. He knew better though. "Nope, I'm coming with you. You're going home, right?"

"You … wanna come home with me?" His voice came

out rougher than he'd intended.

She didn't answer, she just stared ahead of her.

Damn, infuriating woman.

He was not doing this with her. If she wanted to stay in the truck, then fine. He wasn't about to change his plans for her. He was going home, putting his feet up, and he'd be damned if he was going to give her a lift home when she asked.

This was their second drive together. The second one in silence. But this time he was the one on edge. Every few minutes he'd chance a glance over at her, and the crazy-ass woman looked like she didn't have a care in the world.

What the hell is she playing at?

Pulling up to his house ten minutes later, he cut the engine. No one had been here before. Not even Jake. It wasn't that he was ashamed of the place, it just wasn't quite guest-ready yet. When he moved back to Bluestone, he wanted to buy a piece of land to call his own. But being the small town that it was, there wasn't exactly an array of real estate for him to choose from. Which meant he had to settle for a fixer-upper.

Wanting to help Alice out, he rounded the truck. He was still a gentleman, after all. Most of the time anyway. But as he reached to help, the stubborn woman batted away his hand and jumped down. His eyes were fixed on her as she looked around, so much so, he almost missed the car parked around by the side entrance of his house. That's when he realised it was Alice's car. The sneaky thing had left her car here and then gone to find him. How she got back into town, he had no idea.

She caught him looking back and forth between her and the car, a smile tipping up at the side of her mouth.

"So … you gonna invite me in, Deputy?"

"I don't know what you think you're playing at, darlin'… but I'm not—" He was cut off by a hard shove to the shoulder. One he wasn't prepared for, which forced him to take a step back.

"I swear to God, Brady." Her voice was no longer calm. "You wanna play hardball, we'll play. One way or another, I'm not leaving here until we've done your PT. Now, I would prefer it if we did this the easy way and you invited me inside. But if you're determined to be an arsehole, then we'll do it right here, right now." She gestured around the open field in front of them.

Brady didn't know whether to be impressed or terrified that she'd gone from sweet to scary in a split second. But if she was going to play dirty, so was he.

"Sweetness, if you were interested in getting sweaty with me, then all you had to do was ask."

For the first time ever, he saw a tint of colour tingeing Alice Hart's cheeks. It might make him petty, but those cheeks looked something like victory. He'd affected her. Finally. Because she sure as hell had spent the past month affecting him. In ways he was trying his very hardest to ignore.

"On your back, Brady. We're gonna start with a straight leg raise."

"Pants off too? 'Cause, sweetness, normally I prefer if a girl buys me dinner first."

If steam could come out of someone's ears, he would imagine that right about now, he wouldn't be able to see through the smoke.

"I'm not fucking around, Brady. I've got all night, and I'm not going anywhere."

He shouldn't be so excited about the idea of her spending the night with him, but he was. So, like the mature adult he was, he walked away and headed toward the house. Suppressing a chuckle as he heard Alice loudly grumble behind him. After letting himself in, he went straight for the fridge.

Beer will help me.

She was his shadow. A freeloading shadow who grabbed her own beer and joined him on the couch. But the TV couldn't distract him from the daggers currently being shot into the side of his face.

"I'll make you a deal." It had only taken thirty minutes for her to crack. He was a little disappointed. "I'll transfer you to another physical therapist *if* you tell me the real reason you don't want me working on you."

He thought about that for a minute. A new PT was the goal. It would definitely make things easier, but he still didn't want to go into why he couldn't work with her.

Why not? She's read your record, knows all about your injuries and how you got them. You're not telling her anything she doesn't already know, and this way she doesn't get a front-row seat to watch you fail again.

He took another swig of his beer to try and alleviate some of the tension tightening his insides. "Fine," he said through gritted teeth. He didn't meet her gaze and kept his eyes glued to the television. The last thing he wanted to see was her pity.

"I was career military. A marine. I never saw myself doing anything else. It was the only thing I ever wanted to be. And then ... then this happens." He nodded toward his legs. "I was medically discharged. Seventeen fucking years I gave them. Seventeen years wasted."

He felt the warmth of Alice's hand on his forearm and let the heat sink into him. She was trying to comfort him, but it wasn't working.

"I'm pissed as hell. I don't know how not to be pissed. And, yeah, I'm lucky I didn't lose my leg, lucky I can still walk, but that sure as hell doesn't make me feel any fucking better. So no, I don't really give a shit about PT, 'cause it doesn't matter anymore. I won't ever be able to get back to how I was or who I was. Not with this level of nerve damage."

"Okay," she replied, her hand still firmly in place. "What does that have to do with me being your PT though?"

"You really don't get it?" Removing his eyes from the screen, he turned his head, shocked to see the lack of pity on her face. There might be a small amount of sadness across her pretty features, but it was mostly made up of confusion. "We've spent the past few weeks fighting with each other, Ali. You really think I'd be okay with you seeing me at my most vulnerable?"

There it was. Recognition.

"You think I'd use what happened to you … against you?" A flash of hurt crossed her face.

"Yeah, I do." He regretted the words as soon as they left his mouth, but it was too late. Alice was up and rounding the couch.

"I'll file the paperwork tomorrow. The clinic will be in touch with a new appointment time."

He should have stopped her. He should tell her he didn't mean it. But seconds later she was gone, and the sound of the slamming door reverberated around the room.

Alone again. With more guilt to stew in. Perfect.

***

Alice kept her word and a couple of days later, Brady attended his physical therapy session with a burly man named Steve.

Despite Brady's so-called win, his week hadn't been great. When he wasn't working, he was trawling the haunts where he "accidentally" used to run into Alice. But every time they crossed paths, he wasn't treated to his usual tongue-lashing. Instead, she simply left wherever they were, leaving him to feel like a complete dick. It wasn't exactly doing wonders for his ego.

He'd messed up. He'd hurt her. But for the life of him, he had no idea how to fix it. And if he was being honest, he was a little disturbed at just how much he cared. Just the idea of Alice being upset had his insides twisting in knots.

That's why he found himself at Jake's ranch on a Friday night. He was attending the weekly barbecue that his best friend hosted for his staff and guests in the hope of running into her.

"If you're looking for Alice, she's not here yet. Lily just went to go and get her." Jake gave Brady a hard clap on the back and stood beside him.

"I wasn't."

"Sure you weren't." Jake smirked.

Brady wasn't sure why he was lying to his friend. He already knew why he was here. With Alice refusing to acknowledge his existence, it left him with no other choice but to call Jake.

"So what did you do to piss her off this time? Pull her hair?"

Brady snorted. "You know, the usual. Breathing."

He heard her before he saw her—the girly, melodic laugh hitting him straight in the chest. He looked up, hoping to catch her eye. She was walking toward the fire with Lily, wearing a short sapphire dress with matching blue converse. This was her casual look. That was the thing about Alice, she wore dresses daily, but the shoes gave away her mood.

While he was waiting for her to notice him, he watched her push a glossy, errant strand of hair out of her face and grimace. When she finally caught his eye, the grimace turned into a frown. He could tell immediately that she was plotting her exit, but he wasn't going to let her get away this time. With that in mind, he started toward her.

As soon as he was in earshot, he heard her making her excuses to Lily. Though just as Alice turned away to walk in the opposite direction of him, he caught her arm and tugged her back.

"Really, Brady? You gonna cuff me next?"

"If that's what it takes, sweetness."

Lily cleared her throat. "Um, I'll be just over there if you need me, Ali."

He kept hold of Alice while she continued to scowl. "So. You gonna stop running away and actually stay and have a conversation with me?" he asked.

"And when exactly was the last time we had a conversation, Brady? I don't exactly remember you discussing the state of the Middle East with me in between insults?"

Shit. She's right. All we ever do is bicker.

"Fine. Then let's change that. Stay and … let's talk."

Her twisting out of his hold and stomping away was the only answer he got. *Excellent.* He let out a heavy sigh before following her.

He waited until they were out of sight of the guests before closing the distance between them, but she wasn't stopping. The only thing he could do was place himself physically in front of her in an attempt to stop her in her tracks. Stepping to block her every time she tried to go around him wasn't the most mature thing he'd done that day, but if that's what it took to get her to talk to him, then so be it.

"Brady Mitchell. Get the fuck out of my way before I throat-punch you."

"I don't recommend assaulting a police officer, sweetness."

An adorable growl left her lips. "You just can't take a hint, can you? I have nothing to say to you, Brady. Nothing. I'm done with whatever this is." She motioned between them. "I don't have the emotional energy to deal with your shit anymore. I need some sort of truce."

"A truce?"

"Yeah. If we don't talk, then we won't fight. So, we see each other, we each go our separate ways?"

"No." After having first-hand experience of her walking away from him all week, there wasn't a chance in hell he would agree to that.

"Perfect. We're back to one-word answers. *No.* Just *no.* I don't get any more than that?"

"Has it ever occurred to you that I like talking to you, sweetness? Look, I'm sorry about what happened the other day. I was out of line. I know you wouldn't use my injury against me … I don't know why I even said that."

The lines pinched between her brows, unwrinkled, but

the rest of her features remained suspicious. "Okay ... Well, thank you for the apology, I guess. But you're basically admitting that you enjoy fighting with me."

"And so what if I do?"

If her expression was anything to go by, that was the wrong thing to say.

"I'm not you're personal punching bag, Brady. Someone you can just go around taking your anger out on. Believe it or not, *I* don't enjoy arguing with you. I've actually had enough of guys treating me like shit."

For once, he didn't have an answer or a snappy comeback. There was nothing he could really say to that. That was just sad. Sad that men had treated her like that and sad that she had lumped him in with said men. He didn't stop her when she stepped past him. There was no point. Not until he knew how to fix this.

ISOBEL REED

CHAPTER FIVE

It was Sunday, her supposed day of rest and Alice's phone was ringing again. This time she answered it without so much as a glance at the caller ID. She just assumed it was her mother, likely calling back to finish off her "you need to come home" lecture. But it wasn't her mother's voice at the end of the line this time. It was much worse.

"What the hell do you want, Rob?"

So much for a relaxing day off.

"Um ... I have some news, and I ... and I wanted you to hear it from me first."

"Let me guess. Becky's pregnant. Congratu-fucking-lations. Good luck raising the harpy's spawn—was there anything else?"

"Ali, please. Please don't be like that. How many times do I have to say I'm sorry?"

"Was there anything else, Rob?" she prompted.

He cleared his throat. "Yeah. I got an offer on the flat, and I've accepted. I just need your signature on the paperwork, and then you'll get your half of the deposit back."

"Fine. Email it over."

"Yeah, see, that's why I was calling. I've got a client

meeting down your way, and I was just … uh, I was just wondering if we could meet and you can sign the papers in person."

Is he being serious?

"And why in the hell would I want to do that?"

Her heart was hammering. At least it wasn't from the pain anymore. Now it was just pure unadulterated rage.

"I just … I just don't like the way we left things. We were together a really fucking long time, Ali. Can't you just give me this? Just give me an hour. You don't even need to do anything; I'll come to you. I'll come to Bluestone."

One part of her wanted to tell him that she'd rather gouge her own eyes out. But the other part of her, the side that was trying to do what Lily suggested and heal, that part won out.

"Fine, Rob. Text me the details."

She hung up before he had a chance to reply and slumped so far down into her sofa she was practically laying down. Maybe seeing Rob again would be good for her. Cleansing even. And if it wasn't she could always resort to violence. She didn't have to decide right now, she supposed.

Tonight, a bubble bath wasn't going to cut it. Tonight she needed a big ole drink.

***

For a Sunday night, Mickey's was pretty busy. There was just the one lone table free when she arrived, which she quickly nabbed and lined up her two drinks.

I really need to stop coming here alone. Teddy is going to think I have a problem. I mean, buying two drinks probably didn't help either.

Country music bellowed out of the jukebox as she slurped on her gin and tonic. She looked around at all the smiling faces and suddenly felt a pang of loneliness. It was a new feeling, one that didn't have anything to do with her lack of company.

Deciding to push that particular feeling aside and save it

for later, she gulped down her first drink. When she was halfway done with her second, a familiar face approached her table.

"Care to dance?" Ryan held out his hand.

"What are you doing here?" She matched his wide smile and took hold of his hand, allowing him to pull her up.

"What are *you* doing here? You seem to be making a habit of drinking alone."

She followed behind as he led them to the dance floor. "Yeah, well, I seem to be lacking in the friend's department. It's one of the downsides of picking up your life and moving halfway across the world."

He came to a stop and pulled her into him, strategically placing his free hand on her hip. "I'll be your friend." A mischievous grin overtook his face as he started to sway them to the music.

"Hmm, something tells me that you expect a certain kind of benefit with your friendships."

His eyebrow arched. "Would that be so bad?"

She let out a chuckle. "Probably not, but I think I'll pass all the same."

"Fair enough." He picked up the pace and spun her around. The shock of the twirl caused a slight whimper to escape her lips, making them both laugh.

This is what I need. Gin and dancing. Maybe when I get home, I'll sneak over to Lily's and eat some of her cake too. Yep, that's what I'll do.

"Mind if I cut in?" Her cake daydreams came to an abrupt end upon hearing that deep, raspy voice. *Brady.*

Ryan happily passed her over to him and excused himself. *Traitor.* And so she was left in Brady's arms. His caramel-coloured intense gaze fixated on her as he slowly manoeuvred them around the dance floor.

She was finding it hard to swallow. She didn't like being this close to him. Touching him. She really didn't like the way he was looking at her, either. He looked hungry. Like she was his dinner. No. She definitely didn't like this at all.

"You can't look at me like that, sweetness, and expect me not to do something about it."

"Look at you like what?" *There is no fricking way the man can read my thoughts. He's bluffing.*

His eyes heated, the light brown becoming darker. "You know *what*."

Deputy Douche is not hot. He's a dick. He treats you like crap and lives to make your life miserable. You hate him, Ali. Get a fucking grip.

Internal pep talk complete. Alice decided she needed distance. Distance was her friend. After untangling herself from Brady's arms, she hightailed it across the dance floor. Unfortunately, the damn man, who apparently took great pleasure in manhandling her, caught her outside and hauled her into the alley.

"Woman, for the love of God, will you stop running away from me?"

Being crowded against the cool brick wall gave her some serious déjà vu. His hand was next to her head again and his face was tipped down and just inches away from her own.

"*Woman.* It's *woman* now?"

His eyes narrowed. "Grow up, Ali."

Red. She saw lots of red. It wasn't the comment that did it though. No, it was everything. The way he was looking at her, the way he touched her, the smell of pine mixed with his own natural masculine scent that was currently hitting the back of her throat. She'd had enough. Brady Mitchell needed to fuck right off.

"Me? I should grow up? Are you being fucking serious? If anyone needs to grow up, it's you!"

"Oh yeah?" Even the calmness in his voice pissed her off.

"Yeah. You're the one throwing tantrums, Brady. You're the one mourning the loss of your former career and taking that shit out on me. So you can't be a marine anymore … boo-fucking-hoo. You have no idea how bloody lucky you are. You could have died for fucks sake. You could have been paralysed or lost your damn leg!"

"Oh, that's rich, darlin', coming from you."

"What's that supposed to mean?"

"You're one to talk. Your boyfriend cheats on you, and what do you do? You run away. You quit your job, quit your life, you leave the fucking country! That's some real mature shit right there, sweetness. And you're telling me to grow up?"

"Fuck you, Brady!" She pushed at his chest. The exasperating man didn't even move as she continued to push at his rock-solid chest. "Fuck you!"

He all too easily pulled her off him, clasping both wrists in just one hand. When she finally dared to look up, their eyes clashed. The normally light brown stare was darker than she'd ever seen. His eyes were black, so black they made her pulse quicken.

The longer they looked at each other, the shallower her breathing became and the fuzzier her brain felt. For a split second, his eyes darted to her mouth, and she couldn't stop herself from wetting her lower lip. When her gaze met his, she knew there was no turning back. But she didn't have time to process what that meant before his mouth was crashing onto hers.

It wasn't a gentle kiss. It was angry and out of control. He wanted to consume her, punish her, own her. A quick brush of his tongue against the seam of her lips forced them apart, giving him the access he desired. The deeper he delved, the hotter she burned. She wanted more. She wanted to lose herself in him. Burn in the flames that now engulfed them.

One hand went to his hair as she tugged him closer, trying her hardest to satisfy the new cravings he'd created inside her. Her other hand dragged down his chest, where she traced every hard ridge until she met the hem of his shirt. Reaching under, she let her fingers explore. As soon as she touched his bare skin, his guttural groan vibrated down her throat, sending a shiver through her.

Her brain came back online for a brief moment, but before she could do anything useful with it, Brady's lips were on the move. He pushed aside her hair and buried his head in her neck. His magic mouth kissed, licked, and sucked until she was sure he'd fried every brain cell she had.

Around the time she was ready to strip naked and offer herself to him, Teddy, garbage bag in hand, found them. He tried his best to quietly retreat, but it was too late. Even her lust-filled, foggy brain knew that this was all kinds of wrong.

She was the first to pull back. They were both panting. She caught a glimpse of Brady's eyes but quickly looked away for fear of melting under the heat.

"I … I have to go," she stuttered, still catching her breath.

He didn't move but did allow her to walk away. She didn't look back. She couldn't.

CHAPTER SIX

He hadn't meant to kiss her. Sure, he'd thought about it. What kind of red-blooded man wouldn't wonder what Alice Hart's rosy lips tasted like? Just because she annoyed the hell out of him, didn't mean he hadn't noticed that she was sexy as fuck.

What he really needed to do, though, was to stop thinking about her. Stop thinking of how soft her body felt against his, how sweet her lips tasted, and the tiny whimpers she made that he took great pleasure in swallowing.

Goddamnit.

In an attempt to rid Alice Hart from his subconscious, Brady had thrown himself into his home renovations. Any minute he wasn't on duty, he was trying to work off his newfound energy with some good old-fashioned manual labour.

Finally, he managed to pry the last bathroom tile off the wall. He celebrated by wiping the sweat off his forehead with the bottom of his T-shirt, a T-shirt he wasn't quite sure a wash would be able to salvage. He caught his reflection in the cabinet mirror and winced at what he saw. It had been five days since he'd seen Alice and five days since he'd had a full night's sleep. Manual labour only seemed to help when he was awake. As soon as he closed his eyes, she was there again.

While he contemplated his sorry state, the roar of an engine outside pulled his attention to the window. It looked like an old Ford truck was parking just outside his house.

Who the hell is this?

Not expecting a visitor, he went straight for the stairs, cursing to himself about the fact he needed to interact with another human being on his day off. When he swung the front door open, he stood there frozen for a moment, startled by the sight.

"What the fuck are you doing here?"

Ace chuckled, not in the least bit affected by the anger lacing Brady's words.

"Nice to see you too, brother."

Ace wasn't his biological brother of course, but he was the closest thing Brady had to one. That was probably why being discharged had stung as much as it did. The Marine Corps hadn't only given Brady a career, it had given him a family too.

Before he could answer, Ace had him pulled into a hug and was clapping him on the back. Brady couldn't deny he'd missed his friend. They'd gone from seeing each other every day to months of no contact. That's not to say Ace hadn't called when he could. He had. In fact, Brady had been the one to distance himself from him and his other brothers. Talking to them only reminded him of the life he'd lost.

"Seriously, man, why the hell are you here?"

Ace released him and took his time inspecting Brady's dishevelled appearance. "You think I'd leave you swinging in the wind? By the looks of it, I got here just in time." He shot him a smirk.

"You're fucking hilarious. I'm in the middle of fixing up the house. Get your ass inside so I can have a beer while you explain why you're really here."

Ace followed Brady inside and straight to the kitchen, where he removed two bottles and handed one over. They both leaned against opposite granite countertops as they took their first swigs, the cool liquid easing some of Brady's initial shock.

"Come on. Out with it," he goaded.

Ace simply shrugged. "We're worried about you, man. You've stopped returning our calls. I know what happened hit you hard … but cutting yourself off isn't the answer."

"Oh yeah? So did you come all this way to tell me what the answer is?"

"How 'bout we start by talking to your damn brothers?"

He knew his friend meant well, but the last thing he wanted to do was have a heart-to-heart. So, he did what he did best. Avoided it.

"Listen, man, I need to get cleaned up. Can we have this discussion later?" *Or never.* "I take it you're staying?"

His friend studied him for a minute before clapping him on the back again. "Damn right I'm staying. Go shower. I'm gonna order some food—I'm starved."

***

Last night, Brady actually managed to get some sleep. After his shower, they drank some more beer and ate pizza while Ace caught him up on what was new with his old team. They'd steered clear of any heavy topics, for which Brady was grateful. But today, Ace wanted out of the house. Which was why Brady's nostrils were currently filled with bacon grease as he ate his breakfast in the diner, hoping to Christ he didn't run into Alice.

"You worried Dotty is gonna take you out, brother?" Ace raised an eyebrow at him. "'Cause I reckon you could take her."

No, I'm not worried a little old lady is gonna kill me. But a sexy as fuck brunette might.

"Fuck off," was the only answer Brady was prepared to give.

By the time they were done and filled up on coffee and

pancakes, Brady was itching to get back home. He was in the middle of thinking of how he could convince Ace to spend his leave helping him finish his bathroom, when she walked in. How Brady knew it was her before even looking up was a mystery, but he knew nonetheless.

Ace followed Brady's gaze, turning his head slightly to take in the view. And what a view it was. Alice must have been on her way to work because that was the only time she wore those glorious yoga pants and her cropped tank top. Her dark waves were down and wild, just the way he liked them.

Fuck me, she looks good.

And just like that, all the memories of that kiss—the best kiss he'd ever had—came hurtling back to him.

"Damn. Who is *that?*"

The innocent question shouldn't make him want to beat the living daylights out of his friend, yet it did. A burst of irrational jealousy had overtaken Brady, and he had no idea what to do with it. She wasn't his woman. He had no claim on her.

"Not your concern," he replied anyway as he felt his jaw clench.

Ace's deep, rumbling laugh was loud enough to cause Alice's head to snap in their direction.

Shit. Do I wave? Smile? Apologise for sticking my tongue down her throat?

He didn't manage to come to any sort of conclusion, so he was still staring at her in shock when she turned around and walked out of the diner.

Ouch.

"So ... you gonna tell me who she is and why you look like someone pissed in your Wheaties?"

Brady let out a heavy sigh. He was damn sick of watching Alice Hart walk away from him. "It's complicated."

"I'll bet. I got nothing but time, man." Ace stretched out, casually folding his arms behind his head. "It's your choice. You can tell me about the hot brunette, or we can talk about what happened in the sandbox."

That was how Brady found himself telling his brother all about Alice Hart. He didn't hold back either. He'd already held in these feelings for her for far too long as it was.

Brady started with how she was probably the most infuriating woman he'd ever met, but he also didn't forget to mention how she was the most beautiful one too. Add in how funny the woman was, and the best damn kiss of his life, Brady didn't need his friend to tell him he was screwed. Brady knew it already. Knew it the moment he'd gotten his first taste of her. There was no going back now.

***

They'd made an awful lot of progress on the main bathroom in a very short amount of time. After stripping it bare, it had only taken three days to get it close to functioning again. Thanks to Ace, who had carried on working on it without Brady when he had to go to work. He might have answered the phone sooner if he'd have known just how able and willing his friend was when it came to DIY.

As a thank you, Brady had left the safety of his home and taken Ace to Mickey's for a well-earned drink. It wasn't that Brady was no longer concerned about running into Alice, he was. But he had started to accept the inevitable, and talking to an outsider about it had made him realise a few things.

"It's time. I leave tomorrow. And we need to talk about it."

A full minute passed before any words left Brady's mouth, but Ace's gaze never wavered. His eyes were laser-focused on Brady. He knew it was time. They'd danced around the topic all week, even though he could tell his friend's patience was waning.

After bracing himself for the worst, he met his brother's eyes. "It was my fault," he blurted.

"Come again?"

"It was my fault," Brady repeated, swallowing down the newly formed lump in his throat. "I should've listened to my gut; I knew something was off when we arrived. And now a good man is dead. Because of me."

"You cannot be fucking serious, man? That's bullshit, and you know it. Ricky's death has fuck-all to do with you, and there was no way in hell you coulda prevented what went down."

Brady downed the rest of the whisky he'd been nursing since they'd arrived. "You know as well as I do that instinct is what has kept us all alive. That day ... I fucking knew something wasn't right. It was too quiet. If I'd have just listened—"

"Enough," Ace cut him off. "Don't fucking do that. I think you're forgetting something, brother. I'm the one who sent you on patrol. So, by your logic, it's *my* fault. Is that what you think? Huh? I'm the one who gave the order, and now one teammate is dead and the other injured bad enough to get discharged?"

When Brady didn't reply, Ace continued. "If you think I don't feel responsible, then you'd be wrong. It happened on my watch, man. *My* fucking watch."

It had never occurred to Brady that Ace might feel some of the same guilt he did.

"How do you deal with it? The guilt?"

"I knew what I was signing on for. It don't make me sleep any easier, but I have to accept what happened, learn from it, and move on. Otherwise, it will eat me up. Neither of us can go back, Brady. It's done, and no amount of time wishing we did something differently is going to change that."

Move on. Sure. Easier said than done.

Brady didn't want to tell his friend that he still saw Ricky in his dreams. Or that he still relived every minute of what happened over and over again every night. "I just need some time," he muttered into his now-empty glass.

"I'm leaving you a number of someone you can talk to. I know you rejected it last time I offered, but I really think it will help." Brady's expression clearly spoke volumes. "Don't look at me like that, Mitchell. It's not weak to ask for help. Don't be a fucking fool."

Brady picked up the card his friend had tossed onto the scratched-up table. "Thanks, man, I'll think on it."

Ace sighed. "Okay. Look, if you don't wanna talk to a professional, at least pick up the phone and call me. Can you do that?"

Despite knowing he was unlikely to do so, Brady nodded. Anything to get rid of the disappointment plastered all over his friend's face.

It worked. Ace smiled. Even though it didn't quite reach his eyes, Brady would take it. Although he wasn't so keen on the subject change.

"Okay, enough of the depressing shit. So, when are you planning on making a move on the hot brunette?"

ISOBEL REED

CHAPTER SEVEN

It had been almost two weeks since Alice had temporarily lost her mind and kissed Brady Douchebag Mitchell. So far, she'd done a pretty good job of avoiding him, but tonight, her time was up.

Despite numerous excuses, Lily hadn't let her bail. She'd even gone as far as physically escorting Alice up to the main house to where this little get-together was being held.

She'd been in the kitchen, draining her sister's wine for at least an hour, before he arrived. And now he was here, in front of her, and she was suddenly glad she'd been drinking the good stuff.

"Sweetness," he greeted before stalking toward her, "you're looking mighty fine tonight."

She backed away as he continued advancing. It wasn't until her arse hit the kitchen counter that he halted. He was so close. Too close. Every inhale she took, smelled of pine and him.

Has he been rubbing up against the bloody trees?

"What are you doing, Brady?" She internally cursed herself for allowing her voice to come out so breathless.

"Maybe I wanted another taste." His head dipped down slightly, which meant their lips were now aligned and so close she could feel the warmth of his breath against her.

Where is Lily when you need her?

The kitchen, she'd learned, was just a staging area. The real party was out the back where Jake had set up the barbecue. Unfortunately, this meant she was currently alone with Brady, and she was a tad concerned with the way he was looking at her. Like a predator pursuing its prey.

"Maybe you want a knee in the groin?"

His mouth curved up into a small smile, momentarily breaking the intensity of his gaze. Being this close to him was not good. Not good at all. With him this close, all the memories she thought she'd buried came flooding back.

"Sweetness, I've told you before, if you wanna touch me, all you have to do is ask."

Her heartbeat kicked up a notch. She remembered what he felt like all too well.

"Why are you doing this?"

"Doing what?" The small smile turned into a big grin.

Bastard.

"You know *what*, Brady."

Instead of answering, he closed the distance between them and let his lips brush against hers. It wasn't a kiss, yet her mouth still parted for him. All of a sudden, she had a desperate need for oxygen.

He softly dragged his lips across her jaw, following the smooth line up until he reached her ear, the tickle of his breath instantly sending tingles down her spine. "Even before I got a taste, I knew you were addictive, sweetness. So goddamn sweet. I've been on a sugar high for weeks."

Her sister chose that precise moment to enter the kitchen. But Brady didn't back away. No, the smug man only turned his head in Lily's direction and kept his body pressed against Alice.

"Oh … um." Lily stopped in the doorway, clearly unsure of what to do or say.

"Can you give us a minute?"

Alice could see her sister's shock at Brady's stern

request.

"No. Lily, it's fine. We're done here." Alice shot Brady her harshest glare, which apparently had no effect on him whatsoever, as he stood unmoving. Still too damn close.

"No. We're not done." He addressed her first, and then turned back to Lily. "We'll be out in a sec."

Lily took the hint and made quick work of leaving.

Goddamnit. Motherfucking shitballs.

"Brady, I'm giving you five seconds to back the fuck off, or I'll be making good on my promise of my knee acquainting itself with your balls."

Brady being Brady didn't move. He simply smirked and bent his head down once again. She closed her eyes in an attempt to block out the fire she saw in his.

Stay strong, Ali. He's messing with you. Just don't react, and he'll go away.

Only he didn't go away. He moved until his mouth touched hers again, until both of their lips parted and they were breathing each other in. He didn't take what he wanted, though, he remained still. The only indication that he was affected by what was happening was the heavy, choppy breaths she was inhaling that mirrored her own.

"I want you, sweetness," he muttered against her. "I'm a patient man. I'll wait until you're ready. But mark my words, when you are, I'm taking what's mine."

She wasn't quite sure if that was a proposition or a threat.

As he pulled away, she immediately felt the loss of his body heat. Not that she would ever admit to him or herself how good he felt against her.

Alice didn't dare say anything as he took her in. Her knees suddenly weak, she was grateful the counter was there to prop her up. Once he'd finished perusing her face, he left. No more chitchat, no goodbye, just left her alone. So there she was, standing in Lily's kitchen, trying to figure out what the hell had just happened.

By the time Alice did eventually make it outside, she was none the wiser and Brady was nowhere to be found.

Thank God. He must have left.

Worried her body was at least ninety percent wine at this point, she headed straight for the food. Lily was hot on her heels. To give her sister credit though, she did at least wait until Alice had filled up her plate and taken a seat before she launched into questions.

"What the hell was that back there, Ali? Are you two hooking up?"

Alice let out a very unladylike snort. "No, we're not hooking up. And to be honest, sis, I haven't a fucking clue what that was."

"You guys were practically making out in my kitchen, and that's all I get? Spill, Ali, right now." Her sister defiantly crossed her arms.

Alice got two bites of burger before she replied. "Fine. We might've kissed a couple of weeks ago, but it was nothing, a drunken mistake. This is the first time I've seen him since, and things are still a bit awkward. That's it." She decided that Lily didn't need to know that she'd only had two drinks and was very much sober at the time. It would trigger way too many questions that Alice didn't have answers for.

"You guys kissed?" Lily squeaked. "So Jake was right. All those fights you two have, they're like some sort of sick foreplay."

"I'm not playing with Deputy Douche's ding dong, Lily, so can we just drop it? We kissed once. We won't be kissing again. End of story."

Lily didn't look convinced, but Alice didn't blame her. Alice hadn't even convinced herself.

***

Alice let out a groan as she looked up to find Brady casually slouched against the doorframe. Ever since the party three days ago, he was back to his old tricks, meaning she'd run into him at least once a day. Thankfully he hadn't initiated any fighting with her yet, but then again, this was only their fifth run-in, so there was still time for him to press her buttons.

This was the first time he'd shown up at her work, and by the looks of it, he had something to say. Something she wouldn't like.

"Hi, sweetness, hope you don't mind me dropping by." He straightened and entered her therapy room. After a glance around, his golden eyes sliced back to hers. "I was wondering if you were free for dinner tonight?"

What? Is he on drugs?

"You're joking, right?" She crossed her arms protectively over her chest.

"Deadly serious, darlin'. You free?"

He's lost his damn mind.

She blinked twice at him before searching for signs of possible head trauma. "You want me to go out to dinner … with you?" she repeated slowly. "Are you okay? Did you fall … get knocked on the head? No, don't tell me, you're Brady's identical twin here to right the wrongs of your brother?"

A deep roar of laughter echoed around the room. A laugh shouldn't be sexy. It really shouldn't.

Stupid frigging hormones.

"I told you the other day, I want you." His voice sounded rougher as he took a step forward while she took a step back. "And I think you want me too."

"Oh really? So because I had one temporary lapse in judgement, you think I'm easy?"

"Sweetness, you are so far from *easy*, it's not even funny."

She scoffed, finally hitting the back of the wall.

We need bigger rooms. Or maybe when Brady is around I need to make sure I'm in a big fucking open space.

This time when he approached, she sidestepped him until she ran out of side space and ended up in a corner next to her therapy bed. She could see the mirth dancing in his eyes. He was finding this all too amusing.

"Brady, this isn't fucking funny! I don't know what the hell is going on. I'm confused, damnit. And you … you hunting me like I'm your next meal is, quite frankly, freaking me the fuck out."

He took a step back and threw his hands up defensively, the smile plastered across his face not slipping. "Okay, Ali, whatever you want. I told you I'd wait, and I'm a man of my word. But just to clear up any confusion, when I say I want you, I want *all* of you. I'm not looking to just hook up. I wanna take you out. On a date. Buy you dinner and talk about the state of the Middle East." She didn't miss the twinkle in his eyes as he repeated her words back to her. "So, when you're ready to do this, you know where I am."

After dropping that bombshell, he turned his tanned, uniform-clad behind around and walked away.

***

Alice was feeling antsy. It was the same feeling she hadn't been able to shake since Brady had told her he wanted her. All of her.

It was Saturday night, and she was alone in her cabin, the TV blaring in the background. Admittedly, staring at the same four walls wasn't helping the situation. But she was too close to running over to Brady's and throwing herself at him, she needed to be locked down. Which is what she was currently doing. Literally locking herself inside a self-imposed prison, under a knit blanket.

Frustrated and bored, she picked up her phone. She needed to talk to someone, someone other than Lily. Someone outside the situation completely.

Scrolling to Lucy's name, Alice hit the call button. Lucy was the closest thing to a best friend she had.

That's what you said about Becky.

Alice flung her head back into the cushions as she listened to the rings. Finally, her friend answered.

"Hey there, Lucy-Lou. You free to talk? I miss you."

"Of course. I just got back from the gym and my legs are officially on strike, so I'm just gonna go ahead and put my feet up."

Alice let out a snigger. "Might as well get a snack too—I got some man trouble, and it's a long-arse story."

Alice laid it all out from the first time they met in Vegas to Brady's impromptu workplace drop-by. Lucy stayed quiet for the most part, injecting some choice curse words every now and again. When Alice was finally done, she waited patiently for her friend's verdict.

"Okay … well, I'm happy to give you my take on it all, but I'm fairly certain you already know how you feel."

"That's the point, Luce, I'm not entirely sure how I feel. I mean, yeah, he's hot, but he drives me fricking crazy. It's like he knows exactly what to say and how to say it to get under my skin. I've never met anyone who's triggered me so much."

"And maybe that's a good thing." Lucy paused for a moment. "What you had with Rob was safe. It was all very mature and sensible. You weren't taking any real risks."

"Um, have you already forgotten about the whole 'cheating on me with my best friend' thing, 'cos I sure as hell haven't. Does that fall into your safe, mature, and sensible categories!?"

"Yes, Rob turned out to be a dick. But if he was the love of your life, don't you think you would be a bit more upset about it all?"

Alice couldn't believe what she was hearing. Especially from her closest friend, who had been there and witnessed the fallout of the breakup first-hand.

"I left the country, Luce, and I quit my job—you think that's what a normal person does when they're not upset?"

"No. You quit your job *a month* after the breakup. And you know as well as I do you didn't leave the country 'cos of that fuckface. You left 'cos you were restless, and you missed your sister. The breakup and what happened with

Becky gave you an excuse to leave guilt-free."

Oh my God, is she right? I mean, I know I wasn't happy, but that's just 'cos I missed Lily, right?

"How the hell did you get to be so insightful?"

"I'm hardly Mystic Meg or anything. I just know you, Ali."

She was so lucky to have Lucy in her life. The truth was, Becky's betrayal had hurt so much more than Rob's. Alice had distanced herself from all her friends since then, even Lucy. Thankfully, though, her friend persisted, and right now, Alice was truly grateful she did.

"Okay, Luce. The floor is yours. What is it that I already feel, and what do you think I should do about Brady?"

"You want him. You know you do. So take him. Give yourself this."

Yep, that's what I thought she'd say. Why is the thought making my hands sweat?

"He wants *all of me* apparently. I'm pretty sure that means some sort of relationship?"

"So? It really doesn't matter what he wants. It's about what *you* want. Make your own rules, Ali. If you want casual, tell him that. I hardly think he's gonna turn you down."

Her friend was right. She could absolutely do this. Screw being safe and sensible. If she wanted Brady Mitchell, then she was going to take him. Her way.

CHAPTER EIGHT

It was a Saturday night, and like the anti-social loser he was, Brady was drinking beer on his couch watching serial killer documentaries. Jake had tried several times to drag Brady out, but he was too pissed to be decent company.

He'd had a long day at work, which had ended with a man he'd stopped for speeding ignoring his warnings and getting into a crash ten minutes later. Brady was now contemplating the idiocy of the general population and shouting at his show every time the victim did something he deemed stupid.

Before he could take his anger out on the television again, someone knocked on his door. The only person who would drop by uninvited was Jake. Brady stayed seated, wondering what the odds were of Jake leaving if Brady just ignored him. Another louder knock sounded out and after mumbling, "I'm coming," he left the comfort of his couch.

What he was not expecting when he flung open the door was Alice Hart, but he couldn't deny how good it was to see her standing there, looking sexy as hell in a short navy dress that clung to all her beautiful curves.

"To what do I owe this pleasure, sweetness?" He couldn't wipe the smile off his face.

"Um … can I come in?"

Never once had he seen Alice nervous, but right there, right then, he realised that that's what she was. He stepped aside and gestured for her to come in, being sure to check out the dress from behind.

"Want a beer?"

She fumbled with her fingers for a moment before giving him a nod. It was safe to say that this was unusual behaviour for Alice. It was kind of freaky. She hadn't even insulted him yet.

Instead, she quietly followed him into the kitchen and leaned against the counter, still looking a little unsure as her eyes darted around the extremely sparse room. Once he'd passed her a beer and she'd taken a sip, she launched straight in.

"So, I've been thinking about what you said the other day, and I'm … I'm ready."

He almost choked on his beer. To say he was surprised was an understatement. He tried his hardest to hide it. What he couldn't stop, though, was his smile stretching even wider, so wide it almost hurt. "Is that right?" All of a sudden, his day was looking up.

She cleared her throat. "I have some ground rules."

"I'm all ears, sweetness."

He took the opportunity to close the distance between them, feeling even more smug when a blush crept up her neck.

"This stays between us. No dates. Only sex."

What the hell? No fucking way!

"I'm not a fan of being someone's dirty little secret, darlin'."

"If you're not interested then …" Alice started to push him away, but he pushed her butt right back against the counter.

"Oh, I'm interested, sweetness," he whispered into her ear, delighting in the quiver it caused. "We'll play by your rules … for now." A groan left his throat as a waft of chocolate and roses hit him. He needed more; he had to taste her. Letting his lips slide down her neck, he nipped and sucked, memorising her reactions as he went. Tonight, he'd turn her into an addict. He would make her crave him just as much as he already craved her.

By the time he'd kissed his way back up to her jaw, they were both panting. He didn't think it were possible for her to look any sexier, until he saw those glossy blue eyes. Taking advantage of her parted lips, he wasted no time claiming her mouth and pushing his tongue inside until he was swallowing her moans. She tasted like beer and toothpaste.

Fucking beautiful.

As he slid his hands over her waist, he could feel his heartbeat slam against his chest. Even through her clothes, there was no mistaking the softness waiting for him underneath. The rest of the world around them melted away as their tongues collided and the kiss became more urgent.

She let her own hands roam over him, one going to his hair while the other pulled him so close he could feel her tremble. His whole body was pulsating. Never had a woman affected him like this before. They were only just getting started, and Alice Hart had already ruined him.

"I need you," he muttered into her mouth, unsure if his words were even intelligible.

Placing her hands at the hem of his shirt, she went about pushing up the fabric. Reaching behind his neck, he momentarily broke their connection to pull the top over his head and throw it on the floor. Her fingers went straight to his chest, each stroke burning through him. It was his turn. He explored her curves until he couldn't take it anymore. Using both hands, he made quick work of pushing her dress up and off. Pulling back, he freed her lips once again so her dress could join his shirt on the floor. And that was when he got his first feel of her silky, smooth skin.

Sweet Jesus.

A feral growl vibrated from his chest and down Alice's

throat. She felt so damn good.

"Wrap your legs around me, baby."

Alice immediately complied. Within seconds she was off her feet, and they were on the move. It was time to take what was his.

***

If he thought he was addicted before, then he had a real damn problem now. Not only was sex with Alice unbelievable, but it was also terrifying. Once, twice, three times, and it still wasn't enough. A part of him was worried that no matter how many times he took her, it would never be enough.

Even though she had insisted on a sex-only arrangement, it was pretty obvious that she'd never done casual before. A fact that he was using to his advantage. At first when he suggested she spend the night, she rightly questioned him. He'd eventually convinced her by telling her it was only so they could rest and repeat.

It was now Sunday, and if he had it his way, she wouldn't be leaving anytime soon. They'd showered together, eaten breakfast together, and were currently drinking coffee together.

His lack of furniture had never bothered him until now. Actually, the general state of his house hadn't bothered him, not until Alice was standing in front of him in his bare kitchen in only a shirt looking like some sort of heavenly goddess. She deserved to spend her time in someplace grander than his hovel. A mansion maybe. Or a castle. Hell, a goddamn palace might do it.

"I'm gonna go get dressed," Alice announced, pushing away from the counter.

"Why would you go and do a thing like that, sweetness?" He took another sip of his drink and attempted to hide his smile behind the cup.

"Because, Brady, I don't fancy driving home in your T-shirt."

"Then don't leave."

"Brady," she warned, "I have to leave at some point. This is just sex, remember? And since we're not currently having any, I should go."

He didn't want her to go anywhere. She belonged there with him. It may be just about sex for her, but he wanted more. He wanted to curl up on the couch with her. Hear about her day. Her life. Everything. Listen to her make fun of him. Laugh at her bad jokes. But she wasn't ready for that. Not yet. So sex it was, for now.

"We can change that." He smirked as he placed his mug down and stalked toward her.

His lips went straight to that sweet spot on her neck while his hands moved under the thin cotton.

"Brady." Her voice was shaky, just the way he liked it. "You can't keep distracting me with sex every time I mention leaving."

"Watch me," he murmured into the crook of her neck as he dragged his mouth away and dropped to his knees.

ISOBEL REED

CHAPTER NINE

Alice had never done casual before, so, granted, she had no point of reference, but she was fairly certain this was not how two people in a casual relationship acted.

It was Sunday night, and she was currently curled up on the sofa, resting her head on Brady's chest. He'd curled his arm around her and had been unconsciously running his fingers up and down her side for a while now. At least she thought it was unconsciously.

It was strange to be at Brady's. The house wasn't anything like she expected it to be. It was less bachelor pad, more country chic. She hadn't had a good chance to look around last time she was here, so she didn't realise the lack of furniture in the living room extended into pretty much every other room too.

It also generally needed to be fixed up. Which was clearly what Brady was doing, if the bedroom and main bathroom were anything to go by. But the rest of the place ... well, let's just say there was still lots more to do. The paint needed a refresh, and the floorboards made more noise than she did, but there was nothing wrong with a work in progress. Sort of like her. Maybe that was why she liked it so much: it had potential.

They were on their third serial killer documentary, and she just couldn't bring herself to move. A part of her knew she should go home and get as far away from Brady Mitchell as possible, but the other part, which was clearly winning, was content to lay there all night. It also didn't help that her legs still felt like jelly, which she was sure he had done on purpose.

"Isn't it a bit of a cliché, a cop who likes watching serial killer documentaries?" she said into his chest.

"If it makes you feel any better, I've been watching them a lot longer than I've been a cop." She could hear the smile in his voice.

"When you were in the Marine Corps did you watch documentaries on war?"

She felt his whole body stiffen as his hand froze.

God, I'm such an idiot. He had a life-changing injury that got him medically discharged, and I'm here joking about his TV taste.

"Sorry," she rushed out, "I don't know why I said that. My brain doesn't always catch up to my mouth."

"It's fine." He went back to stroking her. "It's just still a little bit fresh, y'know?"

"Yeah." She buried her head deeper into him. "You know, if you do ever wanna talk about what happened that day, then I'm here."

Brady dipped his head and planted a kiss on top of her hair. "Thank you, sweetness."

They continued to watch the documentary in silence. Alice lasted about twenty more minutes before her lids were too heavy to keep open, and she peacefully drifted to sleep.

***

"Ali? Ali?" Lily called out to her again. "Earth to Ali, your drink is ready!"

Alice shook her head, trying to dispel the weekend flashbacks that were making appearances at the most inconvenient times.

"Sorry." She picked up her coffee from the counter and followed her sister to the table by the window.

They were at Beano's, one of the only cafés in Bluestone that didn't judge her when she wanted fancy-flavoured coffee. It was probably the trendiest place in town and attracted both locals and tourists. It had that whole hipster vibe going on: exposed brick walls, chunky wooden furniture, and low-hanging lights.

"What's going on with you lately? You're being weirder than usual." Lily asked as she took a seat on a wooden stool.

That's a good frigging question. What the hell is going on with me?

"Nothing. I think I'm still trying to get into the routine of having a job again, that's all." *Lies! All lies.*

Despite the vague answer, her sister gave Alice a pass and didn't press her. Just as Lily launched back into telling Alice more about the ranch expansion, her phone vibrated. Pulling it from her bag, she had to stop herself from smiling when she saw who it was from.

Brady: I miss you, sweetness. Can I see you tonight?

It had only been a few days since she'd woken up in his bed, but during that time, he'd messaged her every day. On Monday, it was to tell her not to make any weekend plans. On Tuesday, it was to let her know he was pulling a double shift, otherwise he would be at her door. And today, it was apparently to make mid-week plans.

Alice: 8 p.m., your place?

She wished she was stronger. She really did. But that man was damn talented.

"Who are you texting?" Lily narrowed her emerald eyes at her.

"Oh, it's Luce. She's having guy trouble."

"Oh yeah? She okay?"

This is my chance.

"Well, actually, she's in this sort of casual, sex-only relationship with this dude, and she's been asking my advice. Have you ever done the whole casual thing?"

Alice already knew her sister hadn't, but that didn't mean

she didn't want Lily's take on it.

"Nah, you know me, Ali. I find it difficult to separate sex and feelings. Is she struggling with that too?"

Yes. "No, it's just she's never done something like this before and wanted to know the rules."

"The rules?" Lily raised a brow.

"Yeah, y'know … is it okay to spend the night? And how much talking is too much talking? Things like that. I've not done casual either, so I'm not really much help. Any thoughts I can pass on to Luce?"

"Hmm." Lily tapped her fingers on her cup as she pondered her answer. "Well, I guess spending the night is okay if she wants morning sex. The talking thing is a bit odd. I don't see the issue with having a conversation with the poor man, I mean, she *is* having sex with him after all." She took a sip of her coffee before continuing. "I'm no expert, but casual or not, it's still a relationship. And just like any other relationship, it's about what makes the people in them happy that matters. So as long as they are both comfortable with what they're doing, I don't think they have to worry about any arbitrary rules."

Alice shifted her weight on the chair, hoping like hell she wasn't blushing. "Thanks, sis, I'll um … I'll tell her that. I think it will really help."

***

Alice didn't know why she was freaking out. She'd seen him naked, and he was now on a very short list of people who'd seen her naked too. Taking a deep breath, she knocked on Brady's door and tried her very best not to look half as nervous as she felt.

"Sweetness," he greeted as he opened the door, "goddamn, you look good."

That smile hit the butterflies in her stomach at full force. She managed a "hey" as he gestured her inside, not taking his eyes off her once.

"Why do you always smell of chocolate?"

"What?" The question caught her off guard.

"Chocolate," he asked again, looking at her like she was the mad one. "You always smell like chocolate."

She let a giggle burst free, momentarily forgetting to be nervous. "Oh ... um ... I think it's my body lotion. I use cocoa butter."

He quietly contemplated her answer and nodded.

It was then that she noticed the smell wafting in from the kitchen; it was amazing. So amazing, her stomach groaned in approval.

"Did you cook?"

His grin widened as he took hold of her hand and led her into the kitchen. "Spaghetti and meatballs. I figured I couldn't go wrong with pasta. Who doesn't like pasta, right?"

Like most sane women without a gluten allergy, she loved pasta, that wasn't the problem. The problem was why he was cooking for her in the first place. It felt a lot like a date.

This is not fucking casual.

But because she was a pasta-loving coward, she didn't say anything and tossed around the idea of telling him after her belly was full.

They sat at the kitchen table, which also looked suspiciously un-casual. He'd put down a tablecloth, laid out cutlery, napkins, and was that a frigging candle? She was definitely going to have to have a talk with him. She was still side-glancing the candle when he placed her plate in front of her. Suddenly, all candle-related thoughts dissipated as her mouth began to water. It was time to dig in.

"Jesus. How did you learn to make meatballs like these?" She was fully aware of the moan of pleasure that escaped her lips.

He let out a chuckle. "Military. There is only so much ramen I can live off, so I had to learn how to cook."

"Your mum didn't teach you?" She didn't know

anything about his family, only that he grew up in Bluestone.

He cleared his throat, his tell-tale that he was uncomfortable. "No, my mom … she wasn't much of a cook."

"Where is your mum now? I never hear you talk about your family." She shouldn't really pry, but the fact that she didn't know all that much about him dawned on her.

He set his cutlery down and took a gulp of his beer before locking eyes with her. "She passed away while I was deployed."

Shit.

"I'm so sorry, Brady."

He waved her off. "It's fine. It was a long time ago. She was my only family. I never knew my dad, and my mom never had any more kids. So, to cut a long story short, the reason I don't talk about my family is because I don't have one. Not in the conventional sense anyway."

It wasn't fine. That was obvious from the pain that misted his eyes. Why didn't she know this about him?

Because you've been too busy hurling insults at him to actually get to know the guy?

That was it, she needed to know more. Lily was right, there were no set rules, which meant there was nothing stopping Alice from doing what she felt was right.

Brady had gone back to eating, totally unaware of the new ache in her chest. "In the conventional sense?"

"Yeah. Jake is like a brother to me, as are the men I served with. I'm lucky that I've made my own family."

A smile crept over her. She was happy he had that. "The guy I saw you with at the diner the other week. Is he one of your surrogate brothers too?"

No longer looking tense, his features lit up. "Yeah. That's Ace. He was my team leader. He's a good guy. Next time he's in town, I'll introduce you."

Next time I'll introduce you. As what? The girl you occasionally bang?

"Does he drop by a lot?"

"No. He was checking up on me."

"Oh." She spooned another meatball into her mouth, needing the spicy courage to push for more information. When she finally finished chewing, she took her opening. "He was worried about you … is that because of your discharge?"

"If I answer, can we change the subject?"

She nodded, twisting more spaghetti around her fork.

"The day I got my injury, another member of the team was with me and … and he didn't make it."

Shit. Did he just say?

Everything was starting to make a lot more sense. He lost more than his career that fateful day, he lost a brother too.

She wanted to know more. Ask him who he lost, how he went, what the circumstances were. But she knew that was it. That was all she was getting. End of story. And he had no intention of elaborating.

ISOBEL REED

CHAPTER TEN

"Jesus Christ," Brady panted, rolling onto his back. "You could make a man lose his goddamn mind." He tucked Alice into his side and coaxed her head onto his chest. His heart was still hammering. If he wasn't ruined before, there was no doubt he was now.

It was the third weekend they'd spent together, and the more time that went on, the more Alice was opening up to him. There was nothing casual about what they were doing. Not that she would ever admit it. Yes, they were having a ridiculous amount of sex, but that's not all they were doing. Brady would cook for them, they'd cuddle on the couch together and watch documentaries, and they'd talk. Not just about superficial stuff anymore, they were beyond that.

"I think you broke me." Alice dragged her fingertips down the length of his torso, leaving behind a trail of goosebumps.

"I didn't hurt you, did I?" A tinge of panic coated his words.

"No." She sniggered. "But I don't think I can do *that* again until you feed and water me."

He lifted slightly to press his lips against the top of her head. "Whatever you want, sweetness. I just need a few minutes, and then I'll make us something to eat."

And he did need those extra few minutes. He was no fool. Alice Hart was naked in his arms, and he was going to enjoy it for as long as possible. He let his fingers glide down her exposed back, the feel of the creamy, satin texture still managing to electrify every nerve ending he possessed.

Damnit. I want to keep her.

"Okay, Deputy, time's up. I need sustenance."

He watched her push herself up and off the bed. Every inch of her was perfect. His eyes wandered over every soft curve before settling back onto those piercing blue eyes. She was smiling at him, knowing full well he was taking his fill of the view.

"Come on, loverboy, you promised me food."

He caught the boxers she threw at him, disappointed when she covered herself with his T-shirt. He reluctantly rose and shucked on sweats sans boxers, that way they wouldn't stay on long once Alice was fed. It was something he'd learned that she was unable to resist. Strolling over to the doorway, he tagged her hand and led her downstairs and into the kitchen. "What will it be, darlin'?"

Alice hopped up on the counter, her bare legs swinging excitedly. A sight that hit him square in the chest. "I want eggs and bacon ... oh and toast."

Brady set to work, unable to keep the grin from his face. Having her here with him just felt so right. If you'd have asked him a month ago if he was in any sort of place to get into a serious relationship, the answer would undoubtedly be *hell no*. But now, that's all he wanted. And there was only one person he wanted it with.

Unfortunately for him, Alice was heavily in the denial stage of what was happening between them. He shouldn't really care, because he was getting all the benefits of a relationship behind closed doors, but he did. Being her dirty little secret was getting old. And continuing to lie to his best friend was getting harder.

"What made you want to become a marine?"

The question snapped him back to reality. They'd always skirted around his time in the Marine Corps when talking. Not that he hadn't told her about the places he'd travelled or the friends he'd made, but it hadn't gone any deeper than that. She'd cottoned on early that it was a sore subject and never pushed.

"It may sound corny, but I wanted to serve my country. When I enlisted, I figured if I didn't like it, then I'd just do my four years and be done."

"But you liked it."

"Yeah. I felt like I belonged, for the first time in my life."

"You never felt like you belonged in Bluestone?"

He rubbed the back of his neck in an attempt to relieve the tension now stiffening his muscles. "Don't get me wrong, I love Bluestone, that's why I came back. But … I guess I never really felt like I fitted in. Growing up, we uh … we didn't have much. My mom did the best she could, but it wasn't easy. And as it's a small town, everyone knew everyone's business, so it was pretty damn hard to hide the fact that I was the poor kid from the wrong side of the tracks."

She took him in, a look on her face he'd not seen before. Something between fury and sadness. Hopping from the counter, she closed the distance between them and lifted her hand to cup the side of his jaw. She let her thumb softly caress his cheek, which immediately caused his pulse to quicken. What was surprising, though, was when his heart started racing, it wasn't for the usual reasons that a touch from her triggered. This felt different. It felt like more.

Pushing up on her tiptoes, she brushed her lips against his. Her kiss was slow and gentle. When his lips parted, she slipped in her tongue, which he met with his own. Setting an unhurried pace, they took their time exploring each other. He savoured every sensation, trying to memorise how she felt, how she tasted, even her rose scent that was currently filling up his lungs.

When she pulled back, they were both breathless. Her

sea-blue eyes were glittering, and he knew in that moment he would do anything for this woman.

"Tomorrow. I want to take you out." She stepped back as if she'd just taken a blow. "It'll be outside of Bluestone, don't worry, no one you know will see you with me."

He had to bite back his anger. Now wasn't the time.

"I can't."

"Sweetness." He softened his tone this time. "No one will see us. I promise. There's something I wanna show you. Please."

"It's not 'cos of that. I'm not worried about being seen with you." *Why did he need to hear that so badly?* "I umm ... I have plans tomorrow that I can't get out of."

"What plans? Weekends are normally our time, darlin'." He reached over and tucked an errant strand of hair behind her ear.

She shifted on the balls of her feet and looked down at the floor. "Rob's coming into town. He needs me to sign some papers. I'm meeting him at Get Pied."

That motherfucker.

Brady knew this was big. This guy was the reason she was here. Not that she talked about him. Anything Brady knew, he'd learned from Jake, and it was only the basics. That they had lived together and he cheated on her with her friend. To be fair, he didn't need to know much more than that.

"Do you want me to come with you?"

She looked at him, a confused expression on her face. "Why would you do that?"

He ran his fingers down her cheek and along her jawline. "To be there for you, sweetness. To make sure you're okay."

"I don't think that's a good idea." Her eyes went to the floor again, and this time he knew what she was thinking.

She's embarrassed to be seen with you, dumbass. She sees you as a booty call, remember?

***

He wasn't going to go in. He really wasn't. But when that designer-suit-wearing son of a bitch tried to touch her, he was no longer in control of his actions.

He'd been watching from his truck, which was parked across the street from Get Pied. Alice had only been inside five minutes, but he could see from here that she wasn't happy.

Not caring what kind of scene he might make, he jumped out of his truck and started toward the café. Alice's eyes swung to him as soon as the bell rang out above the door. It was when he headed in her direction, though, that they widened in panic.

Tough shit.

Brady didn't hesitate to slide into the booth next to her. His arm went straight around her shoulders, and he instinctively tugged her close. After planting a soft kiss on her forehead, he turned back to face a shocked-looking Rob.

"Aren't you going to introduce us, sweetness?" Brady asked Alice, but his gaze didn't waver from the man sitting opposite him.

She cleared her throat. "Brady, this is Rob. Rob, Brady."

"And Brady is who exactly?"

Brady didn't wait for Alice to reply. "Her man."

Rob's eyes narrowed on him. "No offence, Brady, but this doesn't really concern you. Ali and I have some stuff to work out, so maybe you two can catch up later?"

Is this guy for real?

"None taken, Rob, but I think I'll stick around all the same." Brady then turned to face Alice; he needed to check in with her. "Come help me choose a pie, sweetness?"

"Okay." He was sure he saw a glimpse of relief in her eyes before she turned to Rob. "I'll be back in a sec."

Brady and Alice slid out of the booth and went toward the pie display counter. Once he got there, he prepared himself for her wrath.

"I'm glad you're here," she whispered, leaving him in a

state of shock. "It's harder than I thought it would be. So even though I'm kinda mad you didn't listen to me, I'm also kinda relieved you're here."

His heart was aching now. Admitting she wanted him there, that she might possibly need him, that would have been hard for her. He didn't care they were in public, he needed to taste her. Which is what he did next. In front of God and all of Get Pied, he bent down and took his woman's lips. When she kissed him back, he felt like he was ten feet tall.

They returned to their table hand in hand. No pie in sight. But who needed pie when he had Alice Hart? Rob didn't look very pleased, which only seemed to make Brady happier.

He stayed out of the conversation about Rob and Alice's apartment and watched on as she signed the papers her ex had brought along.

As a silent participant, Brady had nothing better to do than observe the man sitting in front of him. He could see why a woman might go for him. He was well-spoken, wore an expensive suit, he probably had a nice car too, and looks wise, he wasn't ugly. He had short dark hair, was clean-shaven, and had some muscle on him, but nothing about him screamed Alice. Brady's Alice wouldn't go for this guy. This guy couldn't get any more vanilla. While Alice, well, she was all fire.

What the fuck was she doing with this asshat?

And as if on cue, the Ali he knew came out to play.

"So, now that you've got some extra cash, you gonna get that surgery that pulls your head out of your arse?" Her expression was so serious, Brady couldn't help but snigger. A snigger he was quick to hide with a cough.

Rob simply rolled his eyes.

"Or … let me guess. Becky is gonna do it for free?"

"Ali," Rob warned, despite there not being anything remotely scary about this man. "Don't."

"I hear she's an expert when it comes to arse play. But

you'd know all about that, wouldn't you?"

Damn. There was that fire.

"I'd watch it if I were you, Ali. That's the mother of my child you're talking about."

Mother of his child? Holy shit.

"Listen, Rob." It was Brady's turn to talk now. "I don't want to have to kick your ass, but if you threaten my woman again, you're gonna leave me no other choice."

"Your *woman*?" Rob's words dripped with disdain. He turned his attention back to Alice. "Where the hell did you find this Neanderthal?"

Her smile told Brady everything he needed to know.

"If you don't want me to insult your choice of partner, Rob, I suggest you don't insult mine. I think we're done here."

Brady took the hint and scooted out of his seat, holding out his hand so he could help her out too.

"Have a nice life, Rob. Oh, and lose my number."

"Ali …"

That was when they left the café, hands entwined, and didn't look back.

ISOBEL REED

CHAPTER ELEVEN

Alice really thought that seeing Rob would hurt like hell, but she'd been wrong. It wasn't like it was all sunshine and rainbows though, either. The first thing that had come out of his mouth was Becky's name, which normally would have pressed her bitch button, but then Brady had shown up. And as much as she wanted to be mad at him for ignoring her wishes, she just couldn't. Because seeing him there, having him next to her, was what she had needed.

It wasn't that it wasn't fun to make Rob jealous; it was. But Brady's presence had given her so much more than that. It was a reminder of the type of woman that she was. She was strong, she was enough, and she was a hell of a lot better off without that cheating scumbag in her life.

"The place you were going to take me to today ... will you take me there?" She turned her head slightly to look over at Brady. His eyes were firmly on the road.

"If that's what you want, sweetness." His normally gravelly voice was gentle.

"It is." She gazed at the road ahead and let out a breath she hadn't been aware she was holding.

They settled into a comfortable quiet during the drive, which she appreciated. She needed some time to sort out all the cluttered crap rustling around in her mind. It wasn't until they'd reached the outskirts of Bluestone that Brady broke the silence.

"Just down there is where I grew up."

She followed his pointed finger to the turning up ahead. A sudden urge to see where a miniature Brady grew up took control of her mouth. "Can you show me?"

Why did she want to see? She had no frigging clue. But for some reason, it felt important. Like he was letting her see a side of him he rarely showed anyone else, if at all.

A grunt was the only reply she was given, which was apparently a *yes* if the flip of his indicator was anything to go by.

The rusty sign declaring they'd entered Happy Vale Trailer Park was evidently a little misleading. As she looked around at the shabby trailers lining the narrow path, she wondered what it must have been like to grow up here. They'd talked about their childhoods, and she had already envisioned what a young Brady would look like, only she hadn't placed him here.

He'd told her he grew up poor, told her he was from the "wrong side of the tracks," but she'd never thought twice about it until now. It shouldn't matter, and it didn't to her, but it obviously did to him. She could tell just by how his demeanour had changed as they'd entered the park. It looked something like shame. And she didn't like that.

"This was our spot." He cut the engine in front of a rusty tin trailer and let out a long breath.

A big patch of brown spotted grass surrounded the camper and, again, she imagined him as a child playing out there.

"How long did you live here?"

"All my life, until I enlisted." His voice cracked slightly as he stared at the sad piece of tin.

"You ever play hide-and-seek here?"

"What?"

"Hide-and-seek. You ever play that here? I bet even I

could win a game here—there's so many places to hide. And I guess there were other kids nearby for you to hang out with too?" She watched as the corner of his mouth tipped up, and for some reason she felt like she'd won something. What she'd won, she had no idea. All she knew was that seeing that smile made her happy.

She decided that if her blabbering had that effect on him, then let the word vomit commence. The potential for embarrassment was a better prospect than seeing any more shame on that handsome face. "When I was a kid, I wasn't allowed out by myself. I guess it was 'cos we lived in the city and my parents thought it was too dangerous. I couldn't even sit in the small patch of grass out the front. There wasn't a back garden, you see—one of the drawbacks of living in London, you don't get much for your money."

He was silent, and for a moment, she was rethinking her plan. When she twisted her neck to look over at him, he was just staring at her. If she'd been eating, this would be about the time she wiped her mouth to make sure she didn't have food all over it.

"What?" Alice asked.

"Nothing." He replied yet, he continued to stare until she arched her eyebrow at him in question. That earned her a head shake before he started the engine back up.

Weird. I'm normally the weirdo.

Although the drive out of Happy Vale was quiet, it wasn't as comfortable as it was before. The air felt slightly thicker. Something had changed, but she didn't know what. Luckily for her overactive brain, their next destination wasn't too far away. It was, however, in the middle of nowhere. She searched around for landmarks as they drove down the bumpy side road, but there was nothing but a slightly sloped field ahead.

Brady parked. Well, as much as you can park up in a field.

"Just so you know, I had this all worked out. I was gonna bring a picnic and a blanket and—"

Alice placed her hand on his thigh and cut him off before he could continue. "I don't need a picnic or a blanket or anything else, Brady. I just want to be here with you. Now, show me why you brought me here."

That was obviously the right thing to say because his slight smile had now turned into a full-blown grin. After leaning into her for a quick kiss, he hopped out and rounded the truck to assist with her exit. She accepted his hand and jumped down. He didn't give her hand back, though, he kept it and began leading her up the field, which she now realised was more like a small hill.

Concentrating a little bit too much on the way Brady's wranglers hugged his behind, she wasn't paying much attention to their surroundings. That is until they stopped. That was about the time her mouth dropped open.

"Holy shit."

"I know, right?"

She didn't reply, she just gawked. The afternoon sunlight illuminated the sandstone cliffs and dipped in and out of the jagged valleys. It was majestic. Breathtaking. But it wasn't just the beauty that kept her in awe. There was something else, something rugged and wild about the sight before them. A little like Brady.

Now you're comparing him to a view? What's next, you gonna wax poetic about his six-pack?

Suddenly needing to sit, she slowly lowered herself into the grass, praying to the sundress gods that she didn't put on a show when she attempted to cross her legs. Brady followed her down and immediately pulled her closer, not caring in the least about the careful, ladylike placement of her dress he'd just ruined.

"Thank you," she whispered as she laid her head on his shoulder. "It's beautiful."

He placed a kiss on her forehead and tightened his grip on her waist. "Just like you, sweetness."

They stayed like that for a while. Quiet. Drinking in the view. And she realised something. Being here with Brady, in this moment, with this view, nothing else mattered. All the anxiety she'd had about seeing Rob again. All the pent-up anger she had for her former best friend. It had all gone. It was nothing compared to how she felt right now. Content. Free. Happy. And it was that feeling that made her want to open up to Brady.

"I didn't move here because of what happened with Rob." She let the confession hang in the air. Brady had tried to ask her about Rob a few times, but she'd shut him down. She wasn't ready. She wasn't really sure why she was now. The only thing she was sure of was that something had changed today.

"Tell me."

She wasn't a fan of commands outside the bedroom, yet she felt compelled to do just that. "I hadn't been happy for a long time. My friend Lucy reminded me of that. I think we were missing that passion, y'know? He was safe and I was ... I was comfortable. When I walked in on him and Becky ..."

"You walked in on them?" Brady didn't disguise his shock very well.

I guess when Jake told him why I moved over here, he forgot to mention that little tidbit.

"Yep. And in case you were wondering, Becky was my best friend at the time. One could say, I lost my shit. I guess most women might run away, start crying, maybe call their mum. Wanna know what I did? I started throwing my books at them. Not just any books, though. Hardbacks."

Brady's body was vibrating beneath her. She could laugh about it now, at the absurdity of it all, but at the time it definitely had been anything but funny.

"I did it until I ran out of books. Then, while they were still naked in *my* bed, I started packing a suitcase."

"You were in the room with them ... packing a suitcase?" She didn't miss the humour in his voice.

"Yep. They were both screaming at me at this point, probably mad about the books, but I blocked it all out. Got my shit and got the hell out of there."

"Jesus, baby." Brady shook his head as his eyes softened.

"Anyway. About a month later, I quit my job. Not because Rob had broken my heart, but because breaking up with him gave me an out. There was nothing keeping me in London anymore, and I felt free. And to be truly free to do whatever and go wherever, I needed to quit my job."

"So why Bluestone, apart from the obvious?"

"Well, sorry to disappoint, but it was the obvious that led me here. I missed my sister. Now that she's married, I know it's only a matter of time before her and Jake start having kids. I don't want to miss out on all that stuff. I want to be close by."

"So Bluestone is it for you? No going back to the city, no going back to England—you're going to stay here forever just to be close to Lily?"

When he put it like that, it sounded stupid. Maybe it was. But if she'd learned anything in her twenty-seven years on this planet, it's that possessions and jobs didn't make you happy, people did. Normally people you love, and it was love for her sister that brought her here.

"Right now, yes."

He placed another kiss on her forehead, and she internally cursed herself for liking it so much. How such a simple gesture made something inside of her twist.

Get your shit together, Ali. Don't make this into something it isn't. It's just sex. Nothing more.

Done sharing, she remembered that she had questions of her own. She just hoped her opening up would allow Brady to do the same.

"Who's Ricky?"

His whole body tensed. As she waited patiently for him to say something, she realised he had no intention of doing so. After untangling from his embrace, she twisted to get a look at him. He looked defeated, but not enough to get her to stop.

"In the night, sometimes … you have nightmares, and

you say his name."

The first time he'd had a nightmare it had freaked her out. She was familiar with PTSD and the types of nightmares that often haunted former soldiers. She knew exactly what his dreams meant. She never said anything before because she didn't have to. He'd never hurt her, he didn't thrash, he just cried out, gut-wrenching cries until she held him, stroked him, and calmed him down.

"I didn't ... Did I hurt you?"

She vigorously shook her head before realising she should probably verbalise it too. "No. Never. There isn't ... You don't thrash or anything. You say stuff though."

She watched as his head dropped into his hands.

I shouldn't have said anything. Good job, Ali. Why don't you punch him in the face while you're at it?

Just when she thought she'd ruined the moment and possibly the day, Brady spoke again. "Remember I told you the day I got my injury another team member was with me?"

Her *yes* was quiet, but thankfully he must have heard it because he continued.

"His name was Ricky. He was a good guy. Married. Had a kid."

Even though she knew where this was going, a heavy knot formed in her stomach.

"My injury, it was caused by shrapnel, an after-effect from the explosion. His though ... he's the one who stepped on it ... on the IED. *Stepped on it*, Ali." The more his voice cracked, the more her heart broke. "There were fucking pieces of him everywhere."

He dug the heel of his palms into his eyes, and she just couldn't take it anymore. Quickly rounding him, she carefully pulled his roughened hands away, revealing his pain-filled eyes. She needed to get closer. Touch him. Comfort him. The way she did at night.

She climbed on top of his splayed thighs until she was straddling his lap. After settling her weight on him, she wasted no time cupping his face in her hands.

There was nothing she could say to make it better. This was all she had. The light kisses started at his jaw and followed the line around his face. When she came full circle and reached his lips, she rested her forehead against his and looked into his caramel eyes. "It's going to be okay."

His eyes closed, and she took the opportunity to brush her lips against his. When he opened, she slid her tongue inside, instantly deepening their kiss. It started off gentle, innocent even, but the longer their tongues glided against each other, the hungrier they both got.

All the raw emotion they'd both kept hidden for so long bubbled to the surface, and suddenly her heart was racing. Her blood heated and all her brain could register was how good Brady tasted. How right he felt.

It wasn't long before he took control of the kiss, pushing his fingers through her hair and holding her face in place so he could take what he wanted.

Before she knew it, his other hand was moving all over her, and when it made contact with the bare skin on her thigh, a familiar fire ignited inside of her.

He drew back his tongue but kept her lips hostage. "I need you, Ali."

Not sweetness, not baby, just Ali. Why those words unravelled her the way they did, she had no idea. It wasn't like he didn't call her Ali; he did, all the time. But in the bedroom, in the heat of the moment, it was only the past few nights that he'd let her name leave his lips.

"Say it again." Her whole body was ablaze.

"I need you, Ali. I need you so bad."

She took his mouth again and pushed under his shirt. She needed him too, and that scared the crap out of her.

CHAPTER TWELVE

"What the hell, Ali?!" Lily screeched as she stormed into Alice's cabin, disturbing the peaceful cup of tea she was in the middle of having.

"Oh, come on in, sis. No, don't worry about knocking. That whole privacy thing is totally overrated."

"You done?" Lily stood in front of Alice's armchair, hands on her hips and looking murderous.

"What's up, Lilypad?" Alice had a general idea, but feigning innocence was as far as she got when she was planning what to do.

"You and Brady? How long has this been going on, and when exactly were you gonna tell me? Do you know how humiliating it is to hear about your sister's love life from Dotty?"

Bollocks. I could lie, tell her Brady was just there to make Rob jealous. Lily will see right through that though. She always knows when I'm lying.

"It's nothing. I don't want to talk about it."

Smooth.

"Well, tough shit 'cos I'm not leaving until you spill." Lily took a seat on the sofa, which was situated next to Alice's chair, and turned her whole body so she could glare at the side of Alice's face.

Great. Fucking perfect.

Wine. Wine will help. Liquid courage and all that. Alice rose and went in search of her stash. When she returned, Lily only scoffed when Alice offered her a glass.

"Okay, so, um, Brady and I *might* have been sleeping together … for a few weeks." There she'd said it. Let the judgement begin.

"But you hate Brady—you guys fight, like all the time. What changed? Are you guys an item? Is he your boyfriend? Is that why he was all over you in my kitchen?" Of course her sister had a million questions. Alice had a million of her own too.

"Yeah, well, turns out we fight less when we're naked. And no, he's not my boyfriend. It's just sort of … casual."

Really, you're sticking with that? It's only sex?

Alice really wished there was a way you could beat your internal dialogue to death right about now. In the three whole days since Sunday, her brain had been trolling her. It wasn't like she was in denial, she was well aware of the shift in their relationship. She was just choosing not to think about it at all, under any circumstances. Brady and her made sense in the bedroom. Not out of it.

Then why does calling what you have "casual" feel so wrong?

"You, Alice Hart, wouldn't know how to do casual if it came in here and slapped you in the face."

She tried not to think about just how true that statement was. "You know that doesn't make sense, right?"

"Bite me."

"Very mature." Alice took a big, long drink of her wine.

"I'm serious, Ali. I know you're all like *I don't want a relationship. I'm gonna expiry date.* But even you're smart enough to know that that's bullshit. You're just afraid of getting hurt again. This ridiculous plan of yours is just a way to try and protect your heart."

"Lily, I really don't want to sit here and analyse my love life. I told you what you wanted to know. Brady and I have been having sex. Really good sex, actually. It's not a long-term thing, and I'm okay with that. He's okay with that too. As far as the public display of affection goes, that wasn't planned. And, in all honesty, I don't know what that means for us. I'm gonna have to speak to Brady, but if he's happy to carry on as is, then that's what we'll do."

"Really good sex, huh?" Lily smirked.

Fricking mind-blowing. "I don't want to talk about it."

"Uh-huh. Okay. But you know everyone in town is talking about you guys, right? I hate to break it to you, but they think you're dating. You really gonna turn around and tell everyone you're just shagging?"

Alice let out an exasperated sigh. Small towns were the worst. Everyone knowing each other's business. She wondered just how long it would take for her to get used to living like this.

"No, I guess not. I don't want Dotty to have a stroke. I need to talk to Brady."

The problem was, she had no idea how to start that conversation. Or if she even wanted to have it. But as panic started to set in, she knew she had to do something. She had to see Brady. Talk to him. Maybe if they just set a few boundaries, less blurry ones, they could continue what they were doing.

And what exactly are you doing?

Damnit.

***

It was Friday night when she finally caved and marched herself over to Brady's. She hadn't even made it into his house yet when his mouth was on hers and his big hands were pushing up her dress.

"Stop. We need to … talk," she managed to get out as their laboured pants filled the air.

Recognising the lust flaring in his eyes was doing nothing to calm her heart rate.

"Okay, sweetness. What do you want to talk about?" His husky voice was nothing short of smouldering, and she found herself momentarily mesmerized by the sight of the heavy rise and fall of his chest.

Snap out of it.

Attempting to redirect her inappropriate thoughts, she shook her head and moved past him. He quietly followed her into the living room, where they both fell into the comfy couch cushions.

"Okay, so, our little scene at Get Pied didn't go unnoticed—apparently, we're famous. Oh and my sister knows we've been sleeping together, which means by default Jake knows too. So, uh … we need to get our story straight I guess?"

"Our story?"

"Yes, our story. The whole town thinks we're dating."

"So?"

"So?" she repeated.

"Yeah, so what? We're together, Ali. So what if the town knows it?"

"But we're not dating, Brady. We're sleeping together. That's it, remember? This is casual, nothing more. But now the whole of Bluestone thinks we're dating and they're gonna start asking questions. We're gonna get invites as a couple—they're gonna try and marry us off!"

She noticed the familiar tick in his jaw as it clenched, his expression granite.

"There is nothing fucking casual about us, Ali, and you damn well know it."

She did. She'd known for a while. But that didn't mean she was okay with it. That she was just going to accept it. Sex was all she had to give right now. And if she was going to keep having it with Brady, she needed some new rules. She stood and started to pace.

"We fucked up. We blurred the lines. I know that now, but we can fix this; we just need new rules. We need to set boundaries." She could hear the desperation in her voice, but she ignored it. "No more overnight stays, no more TV on the couch or meals together."

It didn't take a genius to work out that Brady Mitchell was not happy. Especially when he rose and reached out to grab her arm, bringing her pacing to a halt. As he entered her space, his mouth was a flat line and his narrowed eyes a darker shade of brown than normal. He kept advancing until she could feel the warmth of his breath heating her lips.

"You want me to fuck you and leave … that what you want, Ali? Get off and get gone? Use your body and then kick you out of my house?"

She felt the anger drip off his every word. All of a sudden, she wasn't feeling so brave. Or sure. She felt sick to her stomach. She couldn't do this. Any of this. What they'd been doing had clearly messed with her head, but the idea of them having sex and him not holding her after, them not talking or curling up on the couch together, made it all seem so sordid. Wrong even.

What the hell is wrong with me? I'm more broken than I thought.

She could feel her eyes start to well. She wasn't this girl. She never cried. The first tear trickled down her cheek, but it was caught by Brady's thumb. Another one began to roll, and he got that one too. Soon his palms were enveloping her face as he tilted her head up to meet his gaze.

"Sweetness, you're killing me." Gone was the anger. Back was her Brady. "If you're not ready to label what we have, then we won't. Fuck what everyone else thinks. But I'm telling you now, I'm not gonna fuck you and then let you leave. That's not what we're doing here."

He was right. That wasn't what they were doing here.

All the fight in her was gone. How could she possibly stand there and argue in favour of something she didn't even want? Was it so wrong that she liked what they had? It's like Lily said in Beano's—it's about what makes them happy that matters. They shouldn't have to explain themselves to anyone else.

Way to cave immediately, Ali.

She *was* caving, and while she was at it, she let him pull her into his chest. Melting into him as he held her tight. She wasn't strong enough to give him more, but she also wasn't strong enough to let him go or change what they had. So she just stood still with him.

CHAPTER THIRTEEN

Brady had spent the last hour doing paperwork in his office, and there was still more to go. Just the thought had him heavily sighing out loud.

It had been a long day, the evidence of which was currently strewn across his desk. His tiredness from last night also wasn't helping. He'd downed four cups of coffee already and all it had left him with was the shakes. Talking Alice down from the ledge had affected him more than it probably should. Despite convincing her to stay, he'd spent most of the night awake, holding her tight for fear she'd change her mind.

Deep down he knew she was just scared of getting hurt again. But it was getting harder to deny what they'd become, and, in all honesty, he was getting sick of denying it.

"Knock, knock."

Jake's deep voice pulled Brady from his thoughts. He glanced up to find his friend casually leaning on the doorway, black Stetson firmly in place. The hat shadowed his face, making it hard for Brady to read his expression.

"Jake. What are you doing here?"

Jake pushed up his hat, and Brady was relieved to see a broad grin across his friend's face. "I think you know what

I'm doing here. You and Ali, huh?"

Brady motioned toward the empty seat opposite his desk and waited for Jake to sit. Brady was ready for this conversation ever since Alice had told him news of them was circulating. He'd spent the past few weeks feeling like a dick for sneaking around behind Jake's back, so in a way he was relieved it was finally out in the open.

"Yeah. Me and Ali. Surprise." His flat tone only caused Jake's grin to widen.

"Okay … and why is it I had to hear the news from my wife?"

"Sorry, man. Ali doesn't really want people knowing, so we had to keep it on the down-low." Even hearing himself admit that had his stomach twisting.

"So you're not taking advantage of my sister-in-law then?"

Brady shook his head. "No, man, it's not like that. This isn't just some hook-up for me. I really like her … a lot."

Jake let out a deep breath. "I've known you all my life, Brady, and I know this isn't just some sort of hook-up for you. I know you like her too. Fuck, man, I knew you liked her when you guys were at each other's throats in Vegas. But the real question is, have you told her just how much? 'Cause according to my wife, Ali is under the impression this thing is just something casual."

Jake not wanting to kick Brady's ass was definitely good news. But the fact that Alice was telling her sister that what they had was just sex was pretty damn devastating. He found himself rubbing his chest, as if he could fix the ache that was now forming.

Stop being such a pussy.

He needed to stay strong. Just because she wasn't ready, it didn't mean she wasn't feeling the same things as him. If she wasn't, then she wouldn't have freaked out so much last night. She also wouldn't have threatened to change the rules and then caved so easily when he rejected them.

"Yeah, well, Ali is in denial at the moment." Brady didn't

notice he was dragging his hand down his face until his day-old stubble pricked his palm. "We both know it's more than what she pretends it is, but I guess she's just not ready to admit it yet."

Jake nodded in understanding. "I'm sorry, man, that sucks."

"It is what it is. But one thing's for sure. Now that I have her, I'm not gonna let her go without one hell of a fight." And that was true. Brady wasn't. He knew what they had, even if she didn't yet.

"Just don't hurt her, Brady. She's been through enough." Jake rose from the squeaky plastic chair. "She's basically my sister now, so sister rules apply. If you fuck her over, then I'll have to kick your ass."

Brady let out a chuckle. He had no doubt. Thankfully, the last thing he wanted to do was hurt her. But he had a feeling Alice Hart sure as hell could hurt him. "Trust me, man, I have no intention of hurting her."

"Come to the barbecue on Friday—it's been a while. Bring Ali with you."

"I'll have to check with her and let you know."

Jake headed out of the door laughing, and Brady wondered what he'd said that was so funny. "You do that, man. Check with your woman."

***

Alice had been talking to Ryan for way too long, and for some reason, all Brady wanted to do was go over there, throw her over his shoulder, and get her fine ass away from him. This was not jealousy. Brady didn't get jealous. He just wanted to take her home, that was all.

When he had suggested they attend the ranch barbecue tonight, he'd assumed that she would be by his side, that they would be together ... in public. It's not like they needed to keep what they were a secret anymore. But the stubborn woman would not even look his way. He was sick of it. And after spending the past ten minutes watching Ryan flirt with his woman, he was also pissed.

Downing the rest of his beer, Brady slammed the bottle on the picnic table before storming over to the firepit. The first thing he did was place his hand on Alice's waist and tug her to his side. The second thing he did was drop a kiss on her lips. The final thing he did was stare down Ryan.

You gonna piss a circle around her next?

"Brady. Good to see you." Ryan smirked. "I guess the rumours are true—you two are together?"

"Yeah, we're together, have been for a while." Brady kept his eyes on Ryan, hopefully conveying a convincing back-off vibe while ignoring the fidgeting Alice was doing underneath his hold.

"Jesus, Brady, caveman much?" She wiggled away from him. "Excuse us, Ryan, we need to go over the details of the big flashing neon sign Brady wants me to wear around my neck."

Brady let her drag him away and around the side of the main house. It was the nearest they would get to any privacy while everyone was outside.

"What are you doing?" She angrily crossed her arms over her chest, apparently waiting for some sort of explanation.

He closed the distance she'd put between them. "What? I can't come over and say hi, give you a kiss? You didn't seem to have a problem with me kissing you this morning."

"You know exactly what you're doing, Brady. You're acting like a jealous boyfriend. And unless there's been a terrible accident in between me leaving your bed this morning and you turning up tonight that has somehow caused you to lose your damn mind ... you'll remember that I, in fact, don't actually have a boyfriend."

"Enough." His tone matched the impatience slowly building inside of him. "Do you even hear yourself, Ali? You were in *my* bed this morning. *My fucking bed.* You think I'm gonna stand here and let some asshole flirt with you?"

"Brady ... I can't—"

She wanted to fight. He could see the blue flames in her eyes. It was her way of pushing him away. But he was over it; they were past this. So, he did the only thing he could think of. He slammed his lips onto hers, effectively rendering her speechless. If she wanted to fight, then this is how they were going to do it from now on.

She pushed at his chest as she broke her lips away. "We can't, not here."

He took her lips again, this time harder, deeper. It didn't matter to him if anyone saw them; he wanted them to be seen. It may make him a caveman, but seeing Ryan flirt with her had been enough to finally make him snap. He wanted everyone to know she was his. What did it matter anyway? Jake and Lily already knew. Their public display of affection had already made its rounds through the town rumour mill. As far as he was concerned, they were officially done hiding.

She pulled away again, slower this time and more breathless. "Brady … I can't … I don't know how to do this."

Goddamn, she is so beautiful. Lips all swollen, hair dishevelled from my fingers, her breath ragged from the kiss. From my *kiss.*

Closing any distance she'd put between them, Brady rested his forehead against hers and used his thumb to trace the moisture on her lower lip. "Sweetness, I hate to break it to you, but we're already doing this. Everyone out there knows. Which means they're not gonna think twice about us making out."

"They think we're something we're not," she whispered.

"Does it matter?" He lightly brushed his lips against hers, testing and teasing.

She surrendered to his touch this time, melting into him. A moan even escaped as his tongue tangled with hers, which only made him feel more desperate. He wanted her. He wanted it all. He couldn't hold back, and the kiss that he thought he was in control of turned urgent.

When her hands wrapped around his neck, drawing him even closer, he knew she could feel it too. The violent pounding of her heartbeat echoed his own. He'd never had this before. Never wanted a woman this much in his life.

"Um ... guys?"

The last thing he wanted was to let her go, but he couldn't very well take her right here on her sister's and his best friend's property. Especially not with an audience. He reluctantly liberated her lips and they both twisted their heads, still close, still panting.

Lily and Jake were standing hand in hand, offering up wide-eyed smiles. Upon sight, Alice released her grip on Brady's shoulders and took a step back. There was a lot of fake coughing until Jake finally spoke again.

"We have an announcement to make, so if you guys are done, would you mind coming back over to the firepit?"

After nodding and a quiet "sure" from Alice, Brady grabbed her hand and they followed Lily and Jake back to the party.

Jake wasted no time garnishing everyone's attention, and Brady had to admit, he was intrigued.

"As y'all know, Lily made me the happiest man in the world some months back by agreeing to be my wife." A round of cheers ensued as Jake took the opportunity to kiss his wife before continuing. "Well, just when I thought I couldn't get any happier or luckier, I was blessed once again. Lily has given me the best gift a man could ever ask for, a baby. Our baby. Who y'all will meet six months from now!"

Cheers, whistles, and hoots filled the air as Alice let go of Brady's hand and ran toward her sister. Brady followed suit and went to congratulate his best friend. His hug was a little more manly though.

"I'm happy for you, man." Brady clapped Jake on the back one last time.

"Thanks, I feel like one lucky son of a bitch, that's for sure."

Maybe Brady did get jealous. The lump in his throat sure as hell felt like it. There was no doubt he was happy for Jake, but this, what his friend had, well, he couldn't help but feel envious. A wife and a child on the way, that's the dream, right? It struck Brady that he hadn't given this particular dream much thought before now.

His attention went back to Alice, her bright blue eyes sparkling, threatening to tear. She was huddled with Lily and Sam, excitement bouncing off each of them. For the first time he let himself imagine what it would be like to have this with her. To have a future. That's when he realised just how far down the rabbit hole he'd stumbled with her. He was in deep. Scary deep. But he didn't want to run for the hills. No. He wanted to pull her down into the hole with him. Make her feel what he was feeling. That they belonged to each other. Right there, he decided to make it his mission. He was going to make Alice Hart fall in love with him.

ISOBEL REED

CHAPTER FOURTEEN

Brady was being weird. Not in a fun, sexual way that she'd enjoy. But in a strange, possessive way that made her want to punch him in the face.

Ever since the barbecue, he'd ramped up his efforts to show the whole town that they were together. It wasn't that she was ashamed of being with him, it was more that she didn't exactly want to shout from the rooftops that her extracurricular activities included using Brady Mitchell's body.

Then there were the questions. All of a sudden, everyone had a vested interest in her future. It's not like she could tell them she was just hooking up with Brady, and the bastard knew it too. So now here she was, stuck in her own web of lies, pretending that she was in some kind of committed relationship. Which was just perfect. It didn't make her want to slam her head against the nearest wall. No, not at all.

"Ali?" Lily's voice snapped her out of her Brady-themed thoughts.

"Sorry, I was listening, I promise. So, your next scan you find out the sex?"

Lily smiled against the rim of her coffee cup. "You were thinking about him, weren't you?"

Despite no customers in sight, Hart's Hardware was not the place where Alice wanted to have this conversation with her sister. When she'd stopped by with beverages, it was to interrogate Lily about the secret pregnancy she'd been keeping from her, not to face the firing squad herself.

"I don't know what you're talking about." Alice left Lily behind the counter and began to roam the aisles.

"You know, when normal people run away from a conversation, they usually try and leave the building," Lily chastised as she followed Alice into the paint aisle.

"And when have I ever been normal, Lilypad?"

"Good point. Now, to save time, why don't you just tell me what's going on with Brady?"

"You *know* what's going on."

"No. I thought I knew, but then I saw you guys making out like horny teenagers in my garden. And let me tell you, Ali, there wasn't a damn thing casual about that kiss, and you know it."

Alice let out a very long, slightly dramatic sigh. More questions that she didn't have an answer for. This thing with Brady wasn't supposed to turn into such a complicated mess. It was just supposed to be fun. A release. An indulgence. Why did anyone have to find out, and why was her sister so damn nosy? "Look, sis, we're hooking up. I hate to break it to you, but kissing is probably the least scandalous thing we've been doing to each other."

"Fine. What about the other stuff then? The hand holding, the general holding of you, and… and all the caveman shit. Brady was putting out one hell of a vibe, which basically said to every other male in the vicinity, *back the fuck off, she's mine.*"

Alice groaned. She knew it. She knew it wasn't all in her head. Taking a big gulp of her hot chocolate, she hoped the sugar would ease some of her newfound tension. "Honestly, I don't really know how to answer that. You have to understand, we've never had to do this stuff in public before. When it was just us, it was simpler. Easier. Now, we have the whole town watching us, and I don't think either of us know how to deal with that. When we're alone... it doesn't matter if he ... or if we ... anyway. You get what I'm saying, right?"

"Okay." Lily said the word suspiciously slow. "So when you're alone I take it you're not having non-stop sex the whole time. You guys must hang out, right? Watch some TV, sleep ...? He probably holds you when you're in bed together or on the couch, that kind of stuff?"

Why does this feel like a trap?

"Yeah, I guess. So?" Alice wasn't sure she was going to like her sister's answer.

"Oh my God, Ali, I love you, but sometimes ..."

Alice didn't get to hear the end of that sentence, because a customer walked into the store. Which was probably a good thing, especially as she was fairly sure she was about to be insulted. This was her chance to escape.

"See you later, Lilypad." She waved as she hurried over to the door before her sister could stop her.

By the time she heard her sister loudly sigh, her feet had hit the pavement.

***

Alice glared at the office landline currently screeching on her desk. Stupid phone was mocking her. She still had a good twenty minutes of her lunch break left, which she planned on spending scrolling through her actual phone.

I knew I should have gone out.

"What's up, Sabrina?" she tiredly answered.

"Hi, Alice, your boyfriend is here to see you, can I send him through?"

Alice winced at the general cheeriness of the receptionist's voice. *Boyfriend? Damn it, Brady.*

"Sure, why not," she sarcastically replied.

This was new. Although they'd run into each other slightly more frequently this week, Brady hadn't shown up at her work before. Well, not since before their arrangement anyway.

The door creaked open to reveal the irresistible tan uniform that might as well have been painted on. But the uniform wasn't the only thing to catch her attention. He came bearing gifts. He was balancing two takeaway cups and a single brown bag.

"Sweetness."

She stood at his greeting and watched as he took a few steps toward her. Once he was close enough, he dipped down to graze her lips with his. She silently cursed her body for instantly craving more. As if he could read her mind, he slowly pulled back, revealing a mischievous smirk and a twinkle in his eyes.

"Later, baby." He winked. "Right now, I have a different kind of treat for you." He handed over one of the cups and the bag. "Hot chocolate with extra cream and one of those brownies you like."

She eyed the items and him suspiciously, unsure of what to make of such a thoughtful gesture. "Okay. Thank you." Those intense brown eyes bore into her, studying her reaction. "As much as I appreciate the diabetes drop, I didn't think we were seeing each other until tomorrow?"

"Yeah, about that, I was thinking I could come over tonight. We've not spent the night at your place before, and I figured now that everyone knows about us …"

"So you wanna do tonight instead of tomorrow?"

"I didn't say that, sweetness." He flashed her that panty-dropping smile. "I said, I wanna come over tonight. Then tomorrow night you'll come to my place. I'm cooking your favourite."

"Brady—" Before she could finish her protest, his mouth was back on hers.

He was sneaky, that was for sure. That magic mouth of his scrambled her brain and left her breathless. Once he was sure she couldn't form a sentence, he released her lips and trailed his mouth along her jaw and down her throat.

"I miss you, baby. I know you miss me too. Say I can come over tonight." He latched onto that sweet spot at the curve of her neck and began to suck.

"You can ... you can come over." She dropped her head back and sighed.

There was no point denying him. Her body wants what it wants.

***

Later that night, all six foot two of Brady Mitchell was at home in her small space. He was also cooking in her tiny kitchen. What they definitely weren't doing, though, was having sex. In fact, she'd received nothing but a chaste kiss since he'd arrived, leaving her more than a little frustrated.

Maybe he's just gone off me. Maybe someone else, someone prettier, someone less difficult has caught his eye.

Whatever was going on, she didn't like it. This wasn't them. Sure, he'd cook for her, but that was at his place, where fewer clothes were involved and way more innuendoes were being flung around. Tonight, he'd shown up with a bag full of groceries and got to work straight away. It felt too domesticated.

"How was work?" Brady looked up from the chopping board, and when their eyes locked, she felt a slug of warmth travel through her stomach, right up to her chest.

"Aren't I the one supposed to be asking you that? Catching bad guys is probably slightly more exciting than me doing some stretches."

Brady chuckled, and that sound did something to her insides too. *Damnit, what's wrong with me?* "Doing some stretches? Is that how you define your career now?"

When she didn't reply, he continued his questioning. "What made you want to become a physical therapist?"

She moved from the couch to the table in the kitchenette. After sitting on one of the red chairs, she pulled her legs up, cradled her knees, and let herself think back to that awful day.

"Well, it wasn't some heroic desire to help strangers, if that's what you think." She paused for a moment, gathering her courage. "When I was twelve I was in an accident, a car accident." Brady instantly turned his back on the stove, giving her his full attention. "I was lucky, really, I mean, it could have been a lot worse. I sustained some injuries and underwent surgery. After that, I had to see a physio." She didn't meet his eye; she couldn't. "I was in a lot of pain for a long time. For a while, I was scared I would never have full mobility in my legs. But Sarah helped me; she was my PT. She changed my life. And I guess she inspired me too. 'Cos after the accident, I just couldn't imagine wanting to do anything else. Be anything else."

She waited for the pity, but instead found herself being hauled out of the wooden chair and pulled into Brady's chest. His brown eyes glistened as he looked into her, possibly seeing too much.

"You're amazing, Ali."

She looked away again, focusing her gaze on Brady's flannel shirt. "Don't do that. There's nothing special about me. If anything, I'm a walking cliché. Little girl needs physical therapy and then grows up to be a physical therapist. I'm a bloody TV movie."

He claimed her chin again, forcing her to face him. "Why do you always do that? Talk down about yourself? Whenever anyone tries to compliment you, you shut them down … usually with some bullshit self-deprecating joke."

I'm not having this conversation. Not with him.

"I think our dinners burning." She knew it was a feeble attempt at avoidance, but it was all she had.

"Let it burn." His stare didn't waver, but his grip did tighten.

Goddamn Brady Mitchell. Goddamn him to hell.

She let out a sigh. "I just … I don't know what to say, Brady. I don't know what you want from me." She watched as his features gentled.

He moved his hand to cup her face and let his thumb caress her cheek. "I want you to see what I see, Ali. A beautiful, strong, smart woman who cares deeper and harder than anyone I've ever known."

Her breath caught, and she was suddenly finding it hard to speak. Damn Brady was messing with her cognitive functions now. This isn't supposed to be what they have. She didn't need heartfelt compliments. She didn't want him to see her. See more. She couldn't and wouldn't let her heart be compromised ever, ever again.

She unpicked herself from his hold and took a step back. "I need to use the bathroom. I'll be back in a minute."

Yes, she was a chicken. And that chicken ran away to the bathroom to hide. Her heart was pounding, and her palms were sweating. She needed to pull herself together and start listening to her head and not her heart.

Because you're scared.

So what if she was? She wasn't ready. And there was nothing wrong with that. Just because Brady was trying to pry more from her, it didn't mean she had to give it to him. It was time to remind him of what they were. What they were good at.

After removing her dress, she shimmied back into the kitchen in only her black, lacy underwear. Heat darkened Brady's wide eyes. Good. She'd had the desired effect. The closer she came to him, the more intense his gaze was. She could almost feel the burn of his eyes on each part of her skin as he examined every inch of her.

"Sweetness ... what are you doing?" His voice was rough.

She ran her fingers up his chiselled chest, pausing over his heart and revelling in the hammering she'd caused. "I want you."

She was airborne less than a second later, her legs wrapped around his waist as he strode toward the bedroom. "Don't think I don't know what you're doing, sweetness." His words came out strained.

"You don't look like you're complaining."

"That's 'cause I've got all night, baby."

He cut off any sort of reply with his lips as he kissed her hard, scrambling her brain cells and making her shake as he lowered them onto the bed.

CHAPTER FIFTEEN

Alice was hiding behind sex. Brady knew it. She knew it. And she knew he knew it. But what the hell was he supposed to do about it? It's not like he could resist her. He was only a man after all. Every time he got close to smashing down those walls, she would take off her clothes. Brady knew this was not the sort of problem he should be complaining about, but it was starting to get ridiculous.

As Alice stirred in his arms, he gave her a gentle squeeze. He'd upped their encounters over the past two weeks, and they were now spending every night together. Right now, he wasn't certain if that were a good thing or a bad thing. He was falling harder while she was still pushing him away. At least emotionally anyway.

But today he had a plan. They both had the day off, and he was going to take advantage of that and whisk her away.

"Morning." Her husky, unused voice stimulated a smile.

"Morning, sweetness." He dropped kisses along her hairline and breathed in her flowery, chocolate scent.

"I should get up. Maybe go see if Lily needs any help at the store." She went to move, but he tightened his hold.

"We have plans, sweetness." She looked up at him, confusion clouding her expression. "You said you wanted to do a trail ride, so I spoke to Jake and he's letting us take a couple of his horses out today."

"You ... what?"

"I'm gonna take you on a trail ride, then I thought we could drive over to Splitrock and try out that new Italian place."

She shifted her body until she was up on one elbow and hovering over him, her soft flesh still pressed into his chest. "Are you trying to trick me into going on a date with you, Deputy?"

"Would I do that?" He knew the look of innocence he was attempting to portray was failing miserably.

"Brady ..." She let out an exasperated sigh. "That's not what we do. I'm not your girlfriend. You don't have to take me on dates or hold my hand in public. Let's not pretend we're something we're not."

Brady flipped them over until she was pinned beneath him and he was settled between her thighs. "Are you seeing anyone else?"

"No, you *know* I'm not."

"Good. Are you planning on seeing anyone else?"

She let out a long breath. "No, Brady, I'm not."

"Good. I don't want you to, the same way I don't want to see anyone else. I want you, Ali. Only you. Believe it or not, I like holding your hand in public, and I wanna take you out. So that's what I'm gonna do, and your stubborn ass is gonna let me."

"Oh yeah ... or what?"

A wicked idea came to mind as he let his fingers trail over her silky skin. "I'm sure I can think of a few ways to convince you, sweetness."

He lowered his head into the crook of her neck and relished in her full body shiver as his lips travelled across her collarbone.

"That's not fair." She panted.

"Life's not fair, sweetness."

***

The trail ride turned out to be a great idea. He'd taken them to the very edge of Jake's ranch where they were currently riding through fields of wildflowers and ponderosa pines. They were headed toward the creek that ran through the property, one of Brady's favourite spots.

Letting the last of the summer heat warm his insides, he drank in a view that was almost as captivating as the woman next to him. Golden tinges on every leaf they passed signified a new season was on the horizon. He'd missed this. So much so, it made him wonder what the hell he'd been doing since he'd moved back. This is where he should have been. This was why he came back. Why he loved Bluestone.

Taking a deep breath, he let the earthy aroma fill his lungs and the faint sound of water lapping against the rocks wash over him. It offered him a comfort he hadn't felt in a while. Casting a glance in Alice's direction, he hoped she felt it too. She was a much better rider than he thought, especially for someone who'd only received a handful of lessons from Sam.

"So, how old were you when you learned how to ride, Deputy?"

Brady smiled at the memories her question triggered as he pulled at Sunshine's reigns, directing her closer to the creek. "Jake's old man taught me, must have been eight or nine."

"That young?"

"Actually, that's pretty old for around here. Most ranch kids learn to ride from the age of three. I'm pretty sure that's when Jake learned. But then again, I wasn't a ranch kid, just good old-fashioned trailer trash." His laugh lacked any humour as the reality of his trip down memory lane started to sting.

"Now whose hiding behind self-deprecating jokes?"

"Touché."

They continued their ride along the river where Brady

silently cursed himself for letting those words slip from his mouth. Today was about Alice. Not him. And certainly not his past. Taking another gulp of the crisp air surrounding them, he sought the same comfort as he breathed in horse, hay, and pine.

It had been a long time since he'd felt insecure about how he grew up. He wasn't that poor, useless kid anymore.

No, now I'm a useless grown man. Kicked out the military, used up, broken. Killer. Maybe that's why she's pushing me away—she knows I have nothing to offer her.

"You okay, Brady? You look like you're about to go all Wild Wild West on me."

He cleared his throat. "Yeah, sorry, just thinking. You wanna stop here for lunch?"

"Sure," Alice easily agreed, a look of concern crossing her pretty face.

Once they found a nearby tree to tie up the horses, he helped her down and went about laying out a blanket. He'd packed sandwiches and sodas, and he couldn't help but feel Alice's excited smile strike his insides as she took her first bite.

"Do you really think of yourself as trailer trash?"

Alice's question took him by surprise, which apparently he didn't hide.

"Come on, Brady, don't look at me like that. You can't just throw something like that out there and expect me not to react."

He made her wait until he took another sip of his soda before he replied. "You saw where I grew up, Ali. You know as well as I do that's what I was."

"Bullshit."

"What?"

"I said, bullshit, Brady. 'Cos you weren't rich you're somehow trash? That's some messed up logic, even for you."

"Let's just drop it, yeah?"

"No." *Damn stubborn woman.* "Not until you understand

that you are so far from trash it's not even funny. As much as it pains me to admit it, you're a good man, Brady Mitchell. Maybe even the best man. So what if you didn't have much money growing up? I think if anything it made you a better person. And maybe, just maybe, it made you work harder, fight for better, value everything a little bit more. I don't think it matters where you come from, what matters is how you let it shape the person you are."

He looked at her. Really looked at her. All that beauty she had inside leaked from every single pore. Every day she found a new way to take his breath away. But the most shocking thing about this all was that she had no clue just how special she was.

"Sweetness"—he leaned in and pressed his mouth to hers—"*you* make me wanna be a better man."

She immediately opened for him and surrendered to his kiss. She tasted like home.

The familiar craving for more eventually caused him to reluctantly pull away. But he remained close, letting his thumb lightly caress her cheek. She relaxed into his touch, and he could see the exact moment she lowered her guard.

"I find it hard to let people in." Her whisper was so quiet, he barely heard the confession. "I'm not good at trusting people."

He continued to stroke her. "Because of Rob?"

"No. Well, he wasn't exactly great for my overall self-esteem, but no not just because of him." Her gaze travelled down to her lap, where she began to fiddle with her fingers. "You know that Lily's my half-sister, right? We have different dads."

Jake had filled Brady in when he'd returned to Bluestone that Lily's dad had run off when she was just five and opened up the hardware store here in town. Inheriting the store was what brought her here from London and Alice had helped keep the store in business by becoming a silent partner. "Yeah, Jake told me."

She nodded. "Well, I saw what her dad leaving did to her

and the lasting effects it had on my mum. Then there was my dad."

She went so quiet he thought she was going to close down again. He waited and simply dragged his knuckles back and forth across her cheek, hoping to give her enough comfort for her to continue.

"He umm … just after the accident, I came home early from a PT session and I sort of … I umm … I found him with someone else. Someone who wasn't my mum."

Jesus Christ.

"Does your mom know?"

"Yeah. I told her as soon as she came home. She was upset that I'd been the one to catch them, but she wasn't all that surprised. I think she knew. I heard them fight that night but then nothing. Nothing happened. Nothing changed. My mum just forgave him. And no one ever mentioned it again."

"Do you think that was the only time?" Brady had a feeling it wasn't.

"No. I don't even think that was the first."

"And Lily, what did she say about all this?"

"I never told her. She had just moved out. It was her first year at uni and I didn't want to upset her, so I just never said anything."

It didn't take a rocket scientist to figure out where Alice's trust issues came from. Lily's dad abandoned her mum and his child, Alice's own dad cheated, and then there was Rob, her prick of an ex, whose cheating not only broke them up but also ruined a friendship.

Brady pulled her into his arms, where she quickly snuggled her head against his chest. "I'm sorry, baby. I'm sorry your dad cheated. I'm sorry you had to go through all that by yourself. And I'm sorry you let someone in and they abused that trust. I wish I could kill that motherfucker Rob."

She snuggled in deeper. "That's the thing. I don't think I let Rob in, not fully anyway. I held myself back from him.

I don't think I knew I was doing it at the time, but I did. Maybe a part of me just always knew I couldn't trust him."

"You lived with the guy. Bought an apartment with him." He was stating the obvious now, but the idea of Alice committing to someone on that level that she didn't even trust didn't sit well.

"I didn't think he would hurt me. It sounds stupid now because he obviously did, but I thought that by holding back I was protecting myself."

Brady wanted so badly to be the one she let in, but a part of him was beginning to question whether he was worthy of her trust. It wasn't that he was worried about fidelity. Despite a lack of relationships, he knew he would never cheat. No, he was scared that he would never be good enough for her. And a part of him couldn't help but think that was why she was so hesitant to label what they had. She deserved the world. What if she knew that he couldn't give it to her?

***

It had been a week since their date and things between Alice and Brady were finally moving forward. Opening up about her past had been the first step to letting him in. They also weren't confined to his house anymore. Some nights he would stay at her place while other nights she would come over to his.

For all intents and purposes, they were a couple. Not that she'd ever admit it. But now that she'd gotten more comfortable with people seeing them together, she had started allowing him to take her out in town. Sometimes for lunch at the diner, other nights they'd have dinner at Mickey's, and he'd even gotten her to agree to a date at the local French bistro next week.

Despite all the progress, he still couldn't shake the feeling that he wasn't good enough.

"One more," Steve bellowed as Brady attempted one

more leg press.

Sweat dripped into his eye, causing him to squint. "Fuck!"

Today's physical therapy session had been the hardest one yet. His mobility and flexibility had almost doubled since he'd first started. But instead of being proud of just how much more his body could handle, he was frustrated. Every muscle ached. He found himself comparing this supposed workout to the ones he was used to as a marine.

"Again," Steve ordered, crossing his bulky arms.

"I can't. No more." Brady had hit his limit. As much as he wanted to do more, be more, everything hurt.

"You can, come on. One more set."

"I told you, I fucking can't." Brady pushed himself off the machine, grabbed his towel, and dabbed the sweat off his brow.

"Brady, come on, we've been through this. You can do more, your body can handle more."

"No, it can't." He didn't care that he was shouting or that the two other people in the gym were now staring at him. "This is it, Steve. This is all I can fucking do. How many goddamn times do I need to tell you!"

Adrenaline had turned to rage, and it was pulsing through him with a vengeance. He was angry as hell. At Steve. At himself. At the damn Marine Corps for throwing him away like seventeen years meant absolutely nothing.

He couldn't contain it anymore.

"Brady—"

Steve's next words were cut off by the crashing of the metal chair slamming against the wall.

Brady's physical therapist didn't look amused. In fact, the big, brawny man looked about ready to kill him. But his mouth apparently didn't get the memo. "Fuck you, man."

"Enough!" That voice he recognised, and it managed to slowly turn his fury from boiling to simmer.

Alice charged straight over to him, but when she reached him, she didn't shout or scream at him like he deserved.

Instead, she calmly placed her hand over his chest that was just about ready to explode. "Brady, baby," she said, her voice soft. "Why don't we get out of here? Let's go to my office for a bit, yeah? Come on." She took hold of his hand, and he silently followed her out the gym without looking back.

His pulse was still worryingly out of control as she locked them inside the therapy room. He started mentally preparing himself for a lecture, but she didn't say anything. She just went to him. The next thing he knew, her arms were wrapped around him as he tried desperately to catch his breath.

"It's okay," she whispered as she let her head lay against him. "It's gonna be okay."

He didn't know how long they stayed like that, but it was everything he needed. She was everything he needed. He realised right then that it didn't matter whether he was good enough for her or not, as if he had the luxury of choosing who he fell for. It was too late. His heart belonged to her. He'd fallen in love with Alice Hart.

CHAPTER SIXTEEN

Brady had been on Alice's mind all night, and she needed someone to talk to about it. She wanted to understand what he was going through. She wanted to help him. Unfortunately for her, former marines were in short supply in Bluestone, which is why she found herself at Mickey's at eleven in the morning.

"Ali, what you doing here so early? We don't open for another hour." Teddy rumbled as he continued to take the chairs down off the tables. He was dressed even more casual than usual and had swapped his signature jeans for sweats.

"Hey, Teddy, I actually came to see you. Don't suppose you could spare a few minutes?"

Teddy's astute eyes took her in. She always saw him as something of an anomaly. He looked like some sort of gruff lumberjack, but when he spoke, if you ignored the rumbly baritone voice, there was something sort of gentle about him.

"Sure, take a seat, darlin'. You want a coffee or something?"

She declined the drink and took a seat at the table nearest the door. Since he was obviously busy, she didn't want to keep him too long. While she waited, she surveyed the room. It was strange being in Mickey's during the day. Everything looked a lot less shiny in the daylight. The wallpaper was a little more tattered than she originally thought, the furniture had definitely been well-used, and the stench of beer was clearly a permanent fixture.

"So, what's up?" Teddy took a seat opposite her and slowly sipped on his coffee.

She decided to jump right in. "Um … you were in the Navy, right?"

One of his dark eyebrows arched. "Yeah?"

"I think … no, I know Brady is having some trouble readjusting to life outside the military, and I was wondering if you had any advice? Like, is there anything you think I can do to help? I mean, I get that the Marine Corps and Navy are different, but I figured there might be some similarities when you leave that kind of life behind."

Teddy was quiet for a moment, his green eyes looking solemn. "I'm sorry to hear that, Ali, but I don't know how much use I'll be. Our circumstances are a little different. I left voluntarily. I'd seen too much shit, lost too many people, and wanted out."

Alice's shoulders automatically sagged. "So you didn't find it hard to readjust at all?"

"I didn't say that. I admit it was harder than I thought it would be, but I guess I was more motivated to make it work because it was my choice to leave."

"So no words of wisdom?"

Please give me something. Anything.

She waited patiently while he took another gulp of his drink. "I guess my advice would be to give him time. Just be patient with him."

"That's it? Time and patience?"

"That's a lot, Ali. Trust me. You being there for him will mean more to him than you'll ever know." Teddy's eyes bore into her, and his signature smirk made an appearance. "Look, honestly, I'm not worried about him. Since he met you … I mean, everyone can see the difference. You make him happy. My guess is that more time with you is only gonna make him happier."

Alice snorted. "I don't know about that, but thank you for the advice." Recognising he was all out of wisdom, she rose from her chair. "Can we uh … can we keep this between us?"

Teddy followed suit and stood too. "Of course. I'm the town bartender, remember? I'm used to keeping everyone's secrets."

Alice let out a snigger. "I get it. You're just one big arse vault, Teddy."

"You know it, darlin'." He winked.

Feeling a little disheartened there wasn't anything practical she could do for Brady right now, she headed for the door.

Like baking him a cake? Like that will fix all his problems, Ali. Stop being an idiot.

"Ali," Teddy called out. She spun around to face him again. "Don't hurt him, okay?"

That felt like a slap to the face. All she could do was nod as she pushed the bar door open.

***

"I spoke to Linda the other day, and she was saying they're looking for another physiotherapist for that football club. She mentioned how perfect you were for the job. They wouldn't even need you to come back for an interview, they can just do one of those video thingamajigs."

Alice pulled the phone away from her ear, so she didn't groan right into the speaker. "Mum, who the hell is Linda, and why exactly is she trying to get me a job at a fricking football club?"

"Don't take that tone with me, Alice. Linda is a lovely woman I'll have you know, and she is going above and beyond putting you forward for this job."

Un-fucking-believable.

Alice sank into Brady's comfy couch and took some solace in the fact he wasn't here to witness this absurd conversation with her mother. One that had been long overdue, seeing as Alice had spent the past few weeks dodging her calls. Which meant poor Lily had been receiving even more calls than usual from their mother.

That reminds me, I should buy Lily a cake or something. To say thank you for taking one for the team.

"Well, thank fuck for Linda." Alice rolled her eyes.

"Language!" her mother scolded.

"Mum, I've told you a million times I'm not moving back. I like it here. I like being near Lily, and in case you've forgotten, I'm gonna be an aunt pretty soon and Lily is gonna need me."

As bad as she felt leaving her mother alone in London, she knew in her heart she needed to be here. Not just for Lily, but for herself too.

"You think I've forgotten? It's bad enough that one of my daughters and soon-to-be grandchild are in another country. But now you? Don't you think I've lost enough to Bluestone County as it is?"

Perfect. Must be time for a guilt trip.

Alice hefted herself out of the navy cushions and strode toward the kitchen. Today's guilt trip was going to be served with a side of something alcoholic. Sadly, her choices were limited. It was beer or whisky.

"Whisky it is," she mumbled to herself as her mother continued to tell her how hard it has been since her daughters had decided to abandon her. Alice knew better though. Her mother wanted her and Lily there so she could distract herself from a life with Alice's dad. It was obvious that her mother wasn't in the happiest marriage. One day Alice hoped her mum would leave. Choose herself for once.

A generous serving later, she returned to the couch and sagged back into the cushions. Just as she was ready to down her drink in one, the chime of keys turning in the front door brought her attention over to the hallway.

Brady's buff body was in view within seconds, sending tingles all over her. He looked so good in that uniform. Last week he'd given her a key so she could let herself in if he got waylaid at work. Tonight was the first time she'd used it. Judging by the smile on his face, he was pretty happy about that.

After returning his smile and a slightly dorky wave, she attempted to wrap up the call. "Mum, I gotta go. Tell Linda thank you for thinking of me, but as of right now, I'd rather shave my legs with a chainsaw than take that job."

"So bloody dramatic."

"Yeah, Mum, I wonder who I got that from?"

Once she'd finally gotten her mother off the phone, she jumped up into Brady's arms, who was still leaning against the doorframe. He picked her up with ease, and she wrapped her legs around him, embracing the warmth engulfing her.

Ever since Alice had stopped second-guessing herself, things between her and Brady had been so much easier. So what if people thought they were in a relationship? And who cares that they do so-called "couple things"? All that mattered was Brady knew where she stood, and he was okay with it.

"What's this I hear about chainsaws and a job?" His grin widened as he squeezed her behind.

"Oh, you know, just your standard run-of-the-mill serial killer job vacancy."

"Is that so?" His chuckle had her own body vibrating in unison.

"Yep, maybe you should handcuff me, Deputy, make sure I don't get into any trouble?"

She knew she wouldn't have to ask him twice. Which was lucky because she had an itch that only Brady Mitchell could scratch.

***

Alice was in the middle of doing the unthinkable. She was cooking. All right, so it wasn't the unthinkable, but it was a big deal. Brady was normally the one who cooked, but as he had been spending quite a bit of time at her place lately, she thought she would return the favour.

She was no Martha Stewart by any means, but she had three solid recipes down. Unfortunately, two of those recipes happen to be for cake, really only leaving her with one. Lasagna.

She'd just placed the dish in the oven when Brady sauntered back into the kitchen, fresh from the shower, wearing only a pair of grey sweats and a filthy smile. His hair was still dripping, leaving beads of water trickling down his bare chest. She couldn't help but beam. He knew exactly what he was doing to her.

"Smells damn good in here, sweetness." He hunted her until her backside hit the counter. "And I'm not just talking about the food."

As if to demonstrate, his nose dived into the curve of her neck and travelled up to her ear, all the while being sure to inhale her scent. As much as she wanted to give in to the goose bumps, she had other plans for him.

"Keep it in your pants, Brady." She swabbed his chest. "We have half an hour until dinner's ready, and I thought we could use the time to have an actual conversation."

"Oh, now you wanna talk, sweetness? That why you accosted me at the door earlier and ripped off my shirt?"

She could feel the heat crawl up her neck. She might have been a little overly eager to see him earlier. The bastard smirked at her reaction and took great pleasure running his knuckles over her heated cheeks.

"Anyway," she changed the subject as she pushed away from the counter, "I thought maybe we could talk about what happened the day you got your injury. You never did tell me the full story. And I think it's time. I want to know, Brady."

Normally this would be right around the time he'd shut

down. So she was shocked when he didn't. Apart from a serious expression overtaking his features, he didn't even flinch at her request. But he did remain quiet. She would give him that. Dragging her fingers up and down his side, she waited patiently for him to speak.

Eventually he cleared his throat. "I think I can do that, sweetness."

She ignored the thickness in his voice and let him take hold of her hand and lead her to the sofa.

"Let's take a seat."

She was nervous. She knew this was going to be hard for him, but it was time. His nightmares were still going strong, and if she was going to help him, she needed to know what happened that day. A part of her also hoped that by talking about it with her, he could start to move on.

Once they were settled, she waited again for him to speak. When he did, she wasn't quite prepared for what he said next.

"It was my fault. Ricky's death could have been prevented. He's dead because of me."

"I don't believe that for one second." She placed her hand over his thigh, which was now shaking.

"We were on patrol. It was routine for us, but I knew something was off. It was too quiet. My gut was telling me to head back to base. Everything inside of me was screaming at me to run. But I didn't. I ignored my instinct, Ali." His pained gaze swung to her, caramel-coloured pools of hopelessness holding her hostage. "A good man is dead because of me. He had a family. A wife who would walk to the ends of the earth for him. She's now a widow. And his kid … his kid will have to grow up without a dad. Never knowing him or the man he was. Or how much his dad loved him. All because of me. All because I kept quiet." His head fell into his hands as the trembling in his legs continued.

"It's not your fault." She closed the tiny bit of distance that was between them and let her fingers carefully unpick his hands from his face. "Do you hear me, Brady? It wasn't your fault."

"How can you say that?" A look of pure anguish creased his features. "Did you not hear what I just said? If I'd have just listened to my gut, Ricky would still be here."

"Brady, baby, look at me." She waited until he lifted his gaze back to her. "You're acting like you pulled the trigger instead of just having some weird feeling in your stomach. There is no way in hell you could have known what was gonna happen that day. No way. It wasn't your fault."

She could tell her words weren't sinking in, and it left her feeling helpless. How could he even think for a second that he was responsible?

"Every night I see his face, Ali. I relive what happened over and over again. The explosion, the blood ..."

"I know, baby." She used all her weight to pull him into her. Thankfully, he didn't resist and came down easily until his head rested on her chest. "Tell me what else. What else do you see in your dreams?"

Teddy's advice was at the forefront of her mind as he told her more about the dreams. He described the look on Ricky's face just before the explosion. The screams that pierced his ears. The smell of death that stuck in his throat. And the horror that was the bloody aftermath. All the while, Alice's heart was at risk of cracking in two. What he saw, what he went through, no one should ever experience.

"It's gonna be okay." Her head dipped until her lips brushed across the top of his head. "I promise you, baby, it's gonna be okay."

Time and patience, she reminded herself. Whatever he needed, she knew she would give him.

CHAPTER SEVENTEEN

"You're right, Lilypad, this is way better than watching the Thor workout video again." Alice took another sip of her gin and tonic, her eyes widening as a shirtless Brady bent over to retrieve the fence wire.

"Right?" Sam squeaked, her gaze never leaving her boyfriend's fine form.

Lily, Sam, and Alice sat in deck chairs overlooking the creek as Jake, Duke, and Brady were working on putting up a new fence. Despite the cool breeze and overcast sky, Alice was convinced she was giving off enough heat to set the field alight.

"You know, when you suggested keeping me company today, darlin', I thought you were actually gonna help, not sit there ogling me and my men like we're pieces of meat." Jake strolled over, addressing his wife with a knowing smirk.

Lily beamed. "Less talking, Jake, more removing of clothes, please. How come Brady and Duke are topless and you're not?"

Jake snorted. "'Cause those two assholes like showing off for their women. There's no need for me to show off, sweetheart, I already got you to marry me, remember?"

Lily scoffed at his wink.

Alice couldn't help but giggle. If someone had told her a few months ago she would be sitting here openly perving over a shirtless Brady Mitchell, she wouldn't have believed them. In fact, she probably would have laughed in their faces. But right now, there was nowhere she'd rather be.

Their sunbathing cover was weak at best, so it was no surprise they'd cottoned on. The gawking kind of gave them away.

Brady shot her a crooked grin as he started toward her. She was ashamed to admit that just the sight of him made her knees weak. At least she was sitting down. It made her realise just how far gone she was. She couldn't pretend it was only her hormones in control anymore, especially after the past few weeks. Not only were they spending every night together, but they'd also opened up to each other, and it had brought them closer than ever.

"Sweetness." Brady's gravelly voice caused the air to rush from her lungs. "Are you enjoying the show?" He didn't bother stopping until he made it to her chair, the scent of pine and sweat filling up her nostrils as he loomed over her, bracing his hands on the armrests of her chair.

Okay, maybe my hormones are still very much in play.

Easily capturing her mouth, his tongue immediately swept past her lips. She just couldn't help letting out a whimper as she slowly melted into him. Memorising every taste. Savouring every tingle. He felt so right.

"Will you guys get a room!" Sam yelled from beside her.

As Brady drew back, he kept his eyes firmly on Alice. "Oh, we'll definitely be getting a room. Won't we, sweetness?"

Yep, I'm fucked.

***

Alice was attempting to fidget her way out of freaking out. Sitting in her boss's office, waiting for Richard was making her twitchy. She felt like a naughty child being called into the headteacher's office.

This was it. He was going to fire her. She knew this job was too good to be true.

If she had known this was going to be her last day, she would have at least washed her hair, and she definitely wouldn't be wearing a T-shirt with *It's going tibia okay* scribbled across her chest.

Looking real frigging professional, Alice.

"Alice, sorry to keep you waiting." Richard's booming voice echoed around the room as he entered. He kept his eyes on her as he took a seat behind his large oak desk.

She didn't know him all that well, but he was obviously a veteran himself. Everything about the man screamed military. As well as the shaved head and his immaculate suits, he was also serious, authoritative, and extremely intimidating.

"No worries." In an attempt to keep a slither of her dignity, she crossed her legs and laid her intertwined fingers over her knee. It didn't make her feel any less of a hot mess though.

"I bet you're wondering why I called you in today?" A ghost of a smile appeared across his slightly withered features.

"Um, yes. Did I do something wrong?" She might as well cut to the chase.

Richard's mask dropped for a second. "No, Alice, you haven't done anything wrong. In fact, I'm very pleased with the work that you've been doing."

Oh thank God.

"That's a relief." She managed a small smile as she started to relax.

"I actually asked you in here today to find out what your plans are for the future. Are you planning on staying in Bluestone?"

She wasn't expecting that at all. But it was a good question and one that she'd been thinking about for a while now. However, her sister's recent announcement had made her decision a lot easier. "Yes, I am. I plan on making Bluestone my home, permanently."

Richard grinned, and she realised that she'd never seen him full-out grin before. He must like her after all. "I'm glad to hear that because a permanent position has recently opened up and I'd like to put you forward for it. Is that something you'd consider?"

Oh my God, they actually want me to stay! Greasy hair, bone pun tops and all!

She fought back the urge to do a happy dance around Richard's office. He would not like that.

"Yes, yes, definitely. I love working here, and it would be an honour to be considered for a permanent position."

"Excellent. Just what I wanted to hear. The position is yours, everything else is just a formality. I'll file the paperwork today and get things started."

"Thank you, Richard, I really appreciate it."

And she did. She never expected to actually find a job in her field so close by, let alone one where she liked both the people she worked with as well as her clients. Working at the VA Clinic had been more fulfilling than she'd ever imagined.

Richard stood, which was her cue to leave. She made sure she thanked him one last time before turning toward the door.

"Oh, Alice." His deep voice stopped her in her tracks, and she twisted her head to see him. "I like the shirt."

She let out an awkward laugh, another quieter thank you, and then scurried out the door.

Once she was back in her therapy room, she got the happy dance out of her system and grabbed her phone. There was only one person she wanted to call right now.

After just three rings, he answered. "What's up, sweetness?"

"Guess what?"

"Um … you're the sexiest woman on the planet?"

Damn. Even over the phone he could make her blush.

"No. But I appreciate the lie. I just got offered a permanent position at the clinic!" Her voice was actually squeaking in excitement.

"Baby, that's amazing! Congratulations!"

"I know, I'm so fricking happy," she gushed. "I mean, one minute I thought I was gonna be fired 'cos I told Duncan to go fuck himself, and the next, they're asking me to stay!"

Brady's bassy laugh rumbled down the line. "Of course you did. Right, I'm swinging by after work and taking you out. Tonight, we're gonna celebrate."

That sounded perfect. She wasn't going to dwell on why he was the first person she wanted to tell and the only person she wanted to celebrate with. Not today anyway. Today she was celebrating. A new start. A new life.

The day flew by after that and it wasn't long before she was climbing into Brady's truck and heading into Splitrock. He'd even brought her over a change of clothes after she confessed she wasn't exactly dressed for a night out.

"So, where is it you're taking me again?" Alice twisted her head just in time to see a devilish grin light up Brady's face.

"I told you already, it's a surprise."

Alice did not like surprises. Which she'd already told him. And he'd ignored. "Give me a clue at least? Will there be food there?"

Brady's throaty chuckle filled the cab. "You think I wouldn't feed you? I don't have a death wish, sweetness. I've seen what you're like when you get hangry."

"So we're going to a restaurant?" Alice ignored the hangry jab and fluttered her lashes his way. "Is it the Italian with those risotto balls I like?"

He laughed again, but gave nothing away. "You'll just have to wait and see, sweetness."

Letting out a frustrated groan, Alice slumped back into her seat.

It was ten whole minutes before she was put out of her

misery, which was very quick to turn into what could only be described as child-like wonder.

"No freaking way!" she exclaimed as her jaw dropped open.

"Way," Brady confirmed. "What do you think?"

What did she think? She thought Brady damn Mitchell could read her like a book. "A carnival?" Her eyes darted to him. "You found me a carnival?"

"You wanted to go to one, right?" Brady's smile slipped as he suddenly looked unsure.

Hell yeah, she did. Something she'd only told him once before when they'd been watching a documentary about a carnival killer. She just didn't think he'd remember or that there would be one so close to Bluestone anytime soon. And one on tonight. Today of all days.

"I just can't believe you found one, running tonight as well!"

Back was his smile. "I was gonna take you this weekend, it's on all week, but after the news you had today, why wait?"

Alice threw herself across the cab and into Brady's arms. Curling into his chest, she felt something she'd never felt before. And it scared the crap out of her.

"Now, they don't have the risotto balls you like," Brady whispered into her hair as he tightened his hold on her, "but I have it on good authority that they have the best corndogs in Montana."

Food was the last thing on her mind right now. She needed a shot. Or five.

***

It was girls' night. Alice, Lily, and Sam were dancing up a storm at Mickey's completely sober. The lack of drinking was mostly in solidarity for her sister's very pregnant state. But Alice wasn't all that cut up about the lack of alcohol. Who needed shots when there were burgers, fries and more fries?

"Three more lemonades, ladies?" Teddy asked as they caught their breath at the bar.

"Please." Alice grinned and then turned to the other two. "Shall we grab a table? I need to sit the next song out, or maybe the next ten."

"I'll grab the one in the corner, you guys get the drinks," Sam announced before flipping her long braid over her shoulder and marching toward the table.

It was a busy Friday night at Mickey's and it felt like the whole town was here. The jukebox belted out country classics while groups huddled around the scratched wooden tables. As she made her way over to Sam, drinks in hand, she spotted Ryan. A familiar smirk on his face as he charmed a young blonde thing. She thought back to Brady and how jealous he'd been of Ryan and couldn't help but smile at the memory.

"What are you smiling about?" Lily obviously noticed.

Alice ignored her sister and took a big gulp of her drink, hoping the distraction was enough for her to let it go. Lily continued to eye Alice as she sat down next to Sam.

"So ..." Sam twisted to face her, and Alice knew this wasn't going to be good. "How are things going with Brady?"

Kill me now.

"Um ... fine."

"Oh no you don't, Ali. We want details," Lily beamed. "It's girls' night—you know the rules. No holding back."

"Yes, but I agreed to the rules under duress. I thought we would all be pissed out of our minds, which is the only proper way to spill one's guts. Instead, I'm here, sober as a church mouse, and you fuckers will remember everything I say tomorrow."

Sam and Lily burst into laughter, and Alice couldn't deny how much fun she was having. Even if she was about to be grilled. It wasn't until Lily moved to Bluestone that Alice fully appreciated just how much she needed her big sister. How much she missed her. Coming here was the right decision. Alice knew that now, more than ever.

"Okay. Fine." She let out an overly dramatic sigh. "What do you wanna know?"

Talking about Brady only made her think about him more than she was sure was healthy. How is it possible that he'd managed to crawl so far beneath her skin that she actually missed him? She'd only left him a few hours ago, yet she still couldn't wait to see him again.

Danger! Danger! You're gonna get hurt.

After her interrogation was complete, Sam enlightened them on the perks of living with Duke. All the while Alice was grappling with her own internal monologue, which was quite frankly being more than a little mean and pretty damn judgemental. Just as she managed to get her thoughts on lockdown, the conversation moved on to Jake, who had apparently been binge-reading baby books.

"Every day he'll reel off these random facts. Today he told me that our baby is peeing in me and then drinking it. I mean, come on! I'm gonna shove those bloody books up his arse if he doesn't cut it out!" Lily scowled, ignoring Alice and Sam's giggles.

Another round of lemonade and fries and they were ready to call it a night. And there was only one place Alice wanted to be.

After waving off Lily and Sam, Alice climbed into her car and began the drive to Brady's. Her belly fluttered the closer she got to his place. She knew it was silly, that she was acting like a teenager with a crush, but she'd have to worry about that later.

When she finally pulled into the gravel driveway, she leapt out of her car and made a beeline for the front door. After fumbling in her bag for keys that she had apparently forgotten, she decided to knock instead. Just moments after the first knock, the door swung open, and she could swear she could hear her heart break into a million pieces.

Standing before her was a beautiful blonde bombshell. Her glossy waves hung over her bare shoulders, and even in yoga pants, she still managed to resemble some kind of divine goddess. Even the woman's damn smile was perfect.

Alice was going to be sick. There was only one reason a stunning woman like this would be answering Brady's door at midnight. She felt like the biggest fool on the planet. She had to get the hell out of there now.

"Stupid, stupid, stupid," she chastised herself on the way back to her car.

How could I be such a moron? Of course he's sleeping with other people. He probably couldn't wait for a night off from me. No wonder he didn't suggest I come over tonight.

Her hands were shaking as she pulled out of the driveway. But she didn't cry. Not yet. Her first priority was to get home, only then would she allow herself to fall apart.

The drive back was done on some sort of autopilot. Before she knew it, she was pulling into the ranch. Heart still hammering, stomach still roiling.

"Fucking Brady Mitchell." It wasn't until she parked up that she let the first tears roll.

ISOBEL REED

CHAPTER EIGHTEEN

"Um, I think I messed up," Laura announced as Brady returned to the living room.

"What do you mean?"

"I answered your door, and, um … it was a woman, and I guess she wasn't expecting to find me here."

Brady's heart stopped. There was only one woman who would be here. His woman. "Long, wavy brown hair, blue eyes, pretty little thing?"

His neighbour nodded and offered up a pained expression. "Sorry, Brady. She ran off before I could explain."

He was on the move before she finished speaking. His heart was beating again now but way too fast for his liking. After rummaging around in a few drawers, he found a spare key and threw it in Laura's direction. "Lock up when you leave, yeah?" He didn't wait for a reply. Within seconds, he was out the door and in his truck.

He spent the whole drive to Alice's praying she was there and she would hear him out. They'd come so far over the past few weeks. Everything had changed. Alice was no longer pulling away. He could swear her feelings were just as strong as his were.

It wasn't hard to imagine what she must have thought when Laura opened his door. A part of him was disappointed she thought the worst, but then the other part understood. After all, she'd only ever experienced the worst.

When he knocked on her cabin door, his hands were shaking from all the adrenaline coursing through him.

"Open up, Ali. I know you're in there."

A muffled "go away" came through the wood. He kept pounding, there was no way he was going to let it end this way. They were both in too deep and cared too much for something so trivial to come along and tear them apart.

Five minutes of relentless knocking later, his hand was aching, but he wasn't giving up. He'd stay out there all night if he had to.

"Brady." The door creaked open just enough to reveal Alice's puffy face. Her eyes were red from crying, and it was the first time he'd ever seen her look fragile. It broke his heart to know that he was the one who'd done this to her. "Please go."

"Please hear me out, Ali. It's not what you think."

A sarcastic "original" came out of her swollen lips before she tried to close the door on him. Luckily, he placed his foot out just in time to halt her.

"Don't. Don't compare me to your ex or any other prick stupid enough to let you go."

A moment later, the door was pulled back and she emerged, fiery sapphire eyes blazing. "You're right, you're not like them. You made me believe that this was different. We were different. You know why I was at your house tonight, Brady? I was there 'cos I missed you. You were all I was thinking about all night. God, I'm so fucking stupid."

She missed me. I was all she was thinking about.

He resisted the urge to pull her into his arms, fully aware he'd take a punch if he tried. "You really think I'd cheat on you, Ali? After all this time, that's the kind of guy you think I am?"

"Well, I guess you wouldn't count it as cheating if we

were never really together."

"Bullshit. If we were never fucking together you wouldn't be crying right now."

"I'm not crying! Fuck you!" She tried again to close the door, this time he pushed past her and took a place inside the cabin entrance. "Get out!" Even through the anger and her attempt to put on a brave face, he could feel the sadness and devastation rolling off her.

No longer able to stop himself from touching her, he took a step toward her and cupped her face. "Ali, sweetness, please," he begged as he watched those beautiful blue eyes swell. "The woman at my house tonight, she's my neighbour, Laura. She stopped by with her husband, Drake, to borrow a generator 'cause their power went out. I was out back with Drake when you came by. I've told you a million times and I'll tell you a million more, I only want you, Ali. Only you."

A solitary tear ran down her cheek, which he quickly caught with his thumb.

"It doesn't matter," she whispered. "Tonight just proved what I already knew. I can't be with you, Brady. I can't do this. We've blurred too many lines. I can't see straight anymore."

The blow hit him hard. His stomach twisted, and for a moment he felt as if someone had ripped out his insides. "You really think I would hurt you, Ali? You think I'm capable of cheating on you, lying to you?"

She pulled away from his hold, a look of defiance plastered across her features. "Yes, Brady, I do. Is that what you want to hear? I can't fucking do this. When that woman opened your door tonight, it broke my fucking heart. I can't—"

He crowded her against the wall, the shock cutting her sentence off completely. He lifted her chin and waited until their gazes were intertwined. "Wanna know why I could never do that to you, Ali? 'Cause I fucking love you." Their breathing became more laboured, but she didn't reply. "Did you hear me, Ali? I love you. I've fallen in love with you. So believe me when I say there is no one else. I don't want anyone else, damn it. You're it for me."

Panic flared in those pretty eyes, and he knew she was getting ready to run.

Goddamnit.

She was the only woman he'd ever said those words to, and her silence was killing him. It wasn't supposed to go like this. It sure as hell shouldn't hurt like this.

Seconds later she was out of his hold and out the door, leaving him wondering if he'd ever be the same again.

***

A groan escaped Brady's lips as he tried to lift his head. Half a bottle of whiskey was definitely a bad idea. Not that he cared that much last night. He just wanted to feel numb.

He still couldn't believe Alice had just left like that. He'd told her he loved her, and she walked away. No, she ran away crying. It was safe to say that of all the ways he pictured that moment, he'd never envisioned it going quite so badly.

No longer numb and pretty damn certain death was just around the corner, he managed to open his eyes long enough to register his current state.

I passed out drunk on the couch. Excellent. I'm a bad fucking country song.

His phone vibrated against the coffee table. Alice was his first thought. Reaching out to grab it, he ignored the throbbing pain in his head.

"Hello." He realised how raw his throat was as soon as he spoke, it almost made him wonder if he'd spent the night swallowing nails.

It probably would've hurt less.

"Brady, hey, it's Chase." Chase. His old teammate. Another one of his brothers. Why was he calling? Chase was more of a text kind of guy. He couldn't even remember the last time his friend had actually picked up the phone to call him. Just that thought had Brady's gut tightening. Something was wrong.

"Everything okay?"

"Um, no, I guess not. I'm calling about Ace … something happened. We're back in Texas, and he's, well … well, he's in the burns unit."

Those words had the same effect as a bucket of ice. Brady immediately rose from the couch, paying no attention to the headrush he was rewarded with. Taking the stairs two at a time, he went straight to his bedroom. "Fort Hood?"

"Yeah, I'll text you the details. You coming out?"

Brady didn't miss the hope in his friend's voice. "Yeah, I'm coming out. I'll try and catch a flight out today." As he spoke, he was filling his duffle bag with clothes. "What's the verdict, he gonna make it?" Just having to ask made him nauseous.

The line went quiet, and he found himself glancing at the screen to check the connection. "He'll make it … but prepare yourself, man, it's bad."

Brady let out the breath he was holding. His friend needed him. His brothers needed him. The state of his heart and his head would have to wait. He needed to get his ass on the next plane to Texas.

***

Chase was right. It was bad. Brady took a seat next to Ace's hospital bed. Burns covered half of Ace's upper body and ran from the side of his face, over his arm and along his ribcage. He was asleep. Apparently the pain meds had knocked him out. Which at least meant Brady had time to think up something comforting to say before Ace woke up.

"Thanks for coming so quickly." Chase's muscular six-foot-four frame filled the doorway. "I don't know how long the rest of us will be able to stay."

Fortunately, Brady had managed to get a flight just a few hours after he'd gotten off the phone with Chase. But it had been a long day, and Brady had a feeling it was going to be an even longer night. Of course, his hangover wasn't helping. Or the pathetic state of his heart.

His old team, Chase, Logan, and Benny, had been there to greet Brady when he arrived. Even though he considered them family, this was the first time he'd seen them since they were beside his hospital bed. Trying his hardest to push those memories away, he focused on his friend. He was worried. They all were. But not just about Ace's condition. They were worried they'd get called back and have to leave him alone. The way they all had to leave Brady when he was recovering.

"Don't worry, I can stay if you guys need to go. I called my boss and cashed in some vacation days."

Chase simply gave Brady a chin-lift, but he could see in his friend's eyes just how grateful he was.

It occurred to him then that he still hadn't heard the full story. "What happened?"

"Car bomb."

Shit.

Chase ran his hand back and forth over his dirty blonde crew cut. "They're gonna push for medical discharge."

Brady turned back to Ace. His friend was going to be pissed. They had all planned on being career military. Being medically discharged was never an option. It was a naïve notion, one that most of them assumed would end in death or desk duty.

"Nurse said he'll be out for another hour or so. We're gonna go grab something to eat in the cafeteria. Come with us?"

Brady's head hadn't stopped pounding the whole day but at least the nausea had waned. "Sure." He stood and followed his friend.

The bright colours in the hospital cafeteria were jarring and doing nothing to help his headache. After picking up a turkey sandwich, the only thing that looked mildly edible, he took a seat with the others.

"It's been a long ass time, bro. How's life on the outside?" Logan's tight smile didn't reach his eyes. He'd obviously been caught up in the same carnage if the stitches across his temple were anything to go by.

"Different." It was the only thing Brady could think of to say. It's not like he could tell them the truth. That life on the outside currently feels like he's being stabbed over and over again in the chest.

Benny cocked an eyebrow. "Ace told us you met a woman."

Of course he did.

Brady took a swig of his Dr Pepper. "Yeah, well, it didn't work out."

"What happened?" Chase asked, clearly sensing a story.

The last thing Brady wanted to do was relive last night, but it wasn't like he had anyone else to talk to about it. And he was too damn tired to try and deflect. He scanned his brothers' faces and came to the conclusion that they could use the distraction. So he laid it all out for them, from his and Alice's initial arrangement to him declaring his love.

While they pondered the guts he'd just spilt, he made short work of finishing his sandwich.

Logan piped up first. "You gotta fight for her, man."

"Yeah, it's obvious she feels the same," Benny agreed.

Chase was next to put in his two cents. "She's just running scared."

For the first time in twenty-four hours, Brady smiled. "Thanks, guys, but as much as I love your confidence, I'm not really sure what else I can do. I mean, I told her I loved her, and the woman couldn't get away from me fast enough."

"And you're good with that? Letting her walk away." Chase's eyes roved over Brady's face.

"Hell no, I'm not good with that. But what else am I supposed to do?"

"Prove it to her. Prove you love her. That you're better than those other asshats," Chase returned.

Brady pinched the bridge of his nose, trying to relieve some of the tension building back up in his head. "Am I though? What do I have to offer her, huh? I'm just another former fucked-up marine."

"I fucking knew it!" Chase slammed his hand hard against the plastic table. "You don't think you're good enough for her, do you? Come on, man, you really think this girl gives a shit you're not a marine anymore? I mean, Jesus, Brady, she fell for who you are, not what you used to do for a living."

Benny and Logan grunted in agreement while Chase continued to glare at Brady. He'd rather rehash last night's painful rejection a hundred more times than have this conversation. Because when it came down to it, he wasn't good enough for her. She deserved the world. Not some weak-ass, broken, former marine with blood on his hands.

"Ricky died because of me. I know it, you know it, Ace fucking knows it," he said through gritted teeth. "I got kicked out of the marines, fucked my knee, and if all that wasn't just damn peachy enough, turns out I scream in my goddamn sleep every night too. Yeah, I'm a real fucking catch!"

After gathering his trash, he walked it over to the bin before storming out of the cafeteria. He knew at least one of his friends would follow him, but he didn't care.

Chase kept a safe distance until they made it outside. Suddenly feeling exhausted, Brady was relieved to see a bench so close to the entrance. Seconds after taking a seat, his friend joined him. Neither of them said anything for a while, until finally Brady couldn't take it anymore.

"Say what you gotta say, man."

"Fine." Chase's tone was firm. "First off, Ricky's death was not your fault. The only one who thinks that it was is you. And, yeah, you might have fucked your knee, but you're one lucky son of a bitch, and we both know it. You could have lost your damn leg, and then where would you be? As for the dreams"—he let out a long sigh—"you think we don't get those? Brother, trust me, it's hard to do what we do and walk away without fucking nightmares. They'll get better, I promise. And you know talking about them helps."

Brady only snorted in response.

"Come on, man, it's fucking killing me seeing you beat yourself up like this. We let you push us all away 'cause we thought you just needed time. But this is some bullshit. You need to get your shit together, bro."

"It's not that easy."

"You talk about it with her? What happened to Ricky."

He thought back to his conversation with Alice, how she'd held him, how every night he woke up screaming, she soothed him back to sleep. He really didn't deserve her. "Yeah," he croaked out. "She's had a front-row seat to the nightmares too."

Chase nodded. "You gotta go after her, man. Seriously. Fight for her for God's sake. You deserve to be happy."

Do I? Is he right? Do I deserve to be happy?

He wanted to fight for her. He really did. Life was too short, and he loved her too damn much to let her just walk away. But his love for her was never in question, what was, was whether he could make her as happy as she made him. And he still didn't know the answer.

He didn't have time to think about that though. Not when his friend needed him. When he was back in Bluestone, he'd go to Alice. Explain everything. But right now, he needed to be there for Ace.

***

Ace was awake when Brady returned with coffee. He could tell straight away that the painkillers were already wearing off as he watched his friend grimace with every movement.

"You know, if you wanted me to visit so badly you could have just called."

"Ha fucking ha."

Brady felt a pang of relief as one corner of Ace's mouth tipped up. He was going to be okay.

"How you feeling, brother?"

"Like a fucking bomb exploded."

"Sounds about right." Brady settled into the seat next to Ace's bed. "Seriously, though, man, how are you really doing?"

There was a moment of silence before Ace spoke. "They're done with me, aren't they?" The pain in his voice twisted a familiar knot in Brady's stomach. It wasn't too long ago that their roles were reversed and he was asking Ace the very same question.

"Fuck 'em. Come to Bluestone. I'll set you up with a place, a job, anything you need, man. Just say the word."

A chorus of curses left Ace's mouth, and Brady could only watch on. He didn't have any sage advice or encouraging sentiments. He only had himself to offer, and that would have to be good enough.

CHAPTER NINETEEN

Alice had spent a good few days going out of her way to avoid Brady until she finally realised he'd skipped town. Where he'd gone was still a mystery. All she knew was that he'd taken some vacation days, turned his phone off, and forgotten to tell anyone where he was going. The sheriff was less than impressed when she demanded Brady's location. Let's just say, she was not going to be on his Christmas card list this year.

Currently in Get Pied, drowning her sorrows in peach pie, she was trying her hardest not to think about him. But, of course, she was failing miserably.

Where the hell is he?

She needed to stop obsessing. It was getting her nowhere. She was the one who walked out on him. She was the one who left. But it was for the best, wasn't it?

Her eyes went back to the pie counter and her heart sank. Flashbacks of Brady kissing her haunted her vision. This is where she found her strength, where he helped her find it.

Goddamn you, Brady Mitchell. Damn you to hell.

She let out a heavy groan and cut herself another slug of pie. This is all she needed. Pie won't hurt her. Pie wouldn't cheat on her or lie to her. She can trust pie. Pie will make her happy. Won't it? Her pie-pondering was swiftly interrupted by a familiar figure bouncing into the booth seat opposite her.

"Hi." The blonde was bright, happy, and altogether pretty damn offensive. "We met the other night. I'm Laura."

Oh, how could I forget?

"Sure," Alice replied, purposefully not rising to her level of cheer.

"Listen, I just wanted to say sorry about the misunderstanding. Brady's a good guy, and I hate the idea of messing things up for him, especially since he was helping me and Drake out."

"It's fine, really." This time there was no hiding the impatience in her voice. Alice did not need to be discussing Brady right now. And as petty as it was, this beautiful creature in front of her had triggered a tsunami of crap that she was now living with the consequences of.

"Okay, well ... I guess I should leave you to it."

Finally, she's getting the message.

Laura stood and hesitated for a moment. "Drake and I would love to have you and Brady over for dinner one night. Just let me know, and we can set something up."

Alice, for the life of her, couldn't understand where this friendliness was coming from. She wasn't exactly giving off the warmest vibes. And yet, pretty, smiley Laura was being nice to her. It kind of made Alice hate Laura a little bit more. The woman was fricking perfect.

Alice tried her best to smile but wasn't optimistic about what her face was actually portraying. Going by the sympathetic look the woman gave her, she hadn't successfully managed one.

Her eyes returned to her half-eaten slice, and she wished for a moment that she could be like Laura. So sweet and nice, not at all broken or bitter. Not like her. Brady's words echoed in her head again.

I love you. You're it for me.

She didn't deserve his love. She didn't deserve him. Why did she have to be so screwed up?

***

"You've been avoiding me." Lily looked Alice up and down as she opened the door for her. Not waiting for a reply, Lily pushed past Alice and headed straight to the tiny sofa where she made herself comfortable.

Alice followed her over and settled down next to her, smiling at her sister's baby bump as she did. She still couldn't believe she was going to be an aunt. "A person who was avoiding you wouldn't have asked you over, Lilypad."

"Yes, now you ask me over. After a week of you ignoring my calls and making up imaginary errands when I come by."

Alice had had no choice but to avoid Lily. When Alice wasn't at work, she wasn't fit for human company. In between ice cream and serial killer documentaries, she was crying her eyes out, and that was the last thing she wanted her sister to witness. But now she was ready. Ready to talk and ready for Lily to listen.

"I assume this is about Brady and why he went on that last-minute vacation?"

Alice drew her legs up onto the cushions and tucked her knees to the side. "He told me he loved me," she blurted. "And I ... I broke it off."

"Oh, Ali." Lily quickly pulled Alice into her arms, and like the baby she was, she succumbed to her tears once again. "You love him, don't you?"

She nodded against her sister's chest. It was the truth. She did love Brady. She'd known for a while, even before he'd said it. But she didn't trust it. How could she?

Managing to gain control of her tears, she straightened and immediately saw the sadness in Lily's emerald eyes. She hoped at least some of it was hormones, otherwise she was the worst sister ever. It was bad enough she was sad. Lily didn't need to be as well.

"I'm afraid to trust it. Trust him. How can I when all the men I've ever known have lied and cheated? If I give him my heart, Lily, he'll break it. I know he will."

Her sister soothingly stroked back Alice's hair. "All the men you've ever known?"

It was now or never. This is why she'd asked her sister over.

"Dad," she whispered. "Just after you moved out. I ... I caught him with someone else. I told Mum but nothing happened."

"Oh, honey." Lily dragged Alice into her embrace again, continuing to stroke her hair.

Alice drank in the comfort. She was so sick of being strong. Not when she felt so broken on the inside. She was going to take this. She needed it.

"Why didn't you tell me?"

Alice simply shrugged in her sisters' arms. Lily didn't say anything else, just held her. They stayed like that for a while until Alice was sure her tears were gone for good this time.

Once she'd sat up, Lily rose and went in search of tissues. After letting Lily wipe down her face, her sister's expression grew more serious. "So, let me get this straight. Dad, Rob, and the assortment of douchecanoes you've dated in the past have you believing you're destined to be cheated on?"

When she put it like that, it sounded slightly pathetic. But Alice couldn't deny that was how she felt.

"Rob was supposed to be a sensible choice. The way I felt for him ... I cared about him, sure. But, Lily, it's nothing compared to the way I feel about Brady. And if Rob hurt me, then I know for sure that Brady could fucking destroy me."

"I understand, you know I do. I mean, look what happened with me and Jake. I set myself up for disappointment from the beginning because I've never known any different. But look at us now. Ali, I'm so happy. *He* makes me so happy. Not giving in to fear was the best thing I've ever done. You can have that too if you let yourself."

Alice shook her head. It was not the same.

"Ali, please listen to me. You really think not being with Brady, not being with the man you're in love with, is gonna hurt less? Huh? 'Cos how you feeling right now, sis?" Alice tried to protest but was shut down. "I'm not done. You're afraid, yes. But are you really going to live life not doing things 'cos you're scared? By not letting yourself have this, you're hurting yourself for no reason. A life lived in fear is no life at all."

Alice *was* scared. She'd been scared ever since Brady had kissed her for the first time. She didn't want to live her life in fear, but changing wasn't as easy as her sister made it sound. Could she really just throw caution to the wind and take such a huge leap of faith?

I'll lose him if I don't.

***

Lily's words were still at the forefront of Alice's mind that evening. Brady had only been gone for a week and she couldn't take it anymore. Whoever said that absence makes the heart grow fonder was a liar. If anything, absence was making her heart bleed out. Even breaking up with Rob hadn't hurt this much.

She let out a sigh as she stared into her fridge. "Hmm … what do my feelings want to eat tonight?"

The only thing that looked mildly tempting was the cheese. Her shoulders slumped as she internally berated herself for not getting enough junk during her last shopping trip. Supermarket Alice was an optimist and had foolishly purchased a load of healthy food that didn't look appealing in the slightest.

Pulling out a can of Diet Coke, she went back to the sofa and snuggled back under her blanket. She was in for another lonely night.

Maybe Lily's right. Being scared to get hurt is hurting pretty damn bad right now.

As if her sister was some sort of mystical mind reader, Alice's phone pinged her out of her thoughts. She clicked on Lily's name and her breath caught.

Lily: Just thought you'd wanna know, Brady is back. Think about what I said. Love you, sis! Xx

Brady is back. Those three words sent tingles down her spine and caused a familiar ache in her chest. She realised right then that this feeling wasn't going to go away. Brady already had her heart. There was no use denying it. The real question was, was she prepared to risk it to be with him?

CHAPTER TWENTY

Ace's injury had been a wake-up call. In fact, the entire week had managed to slap some sense into Brady. Life was short. If he had a chance at being happy, then he needed to go for it. Fight for it.

Although he'd been planning for days what he was going to say to Alice, he had yet to talk to her. Mostly because he knew he only had one shot at this. Which meant he had to get it right. Perfect even, if he had any hope of convincing her to give him a chance.

Seeing his brothers again had been emotional. It had brought up a lot of feelings he'd been trying his hardest to ignore. But after a large helping of support and understanding from his friends, he felt like a new man. A new man who hopefully still had a job.

After getting back last night, he'd decided his first stop today would be the station. Clarkson, Bluestone's sheriff, hadn't been too pleased when Brady had called him from the airport, so he was afraid of what he might be walking into.

He let out a deep exhale before knocking on the office door.

"Come in," Clarkson bellowed.

Brady found his boss behind his desk, shuffling a stack of papers of what was most likely yesterday's paperwork.

"Ah, he finally remembers he has a job." Although sarcastic, there was no animosity in his tone.

Thank God.

"Sir," Brady greeted, a small smile stretching the corners of his lips. "I'm sorry again for taking off like I did. I'm back and ready to work. Wherever you need me."

Clarkson studied him for a moment. "So, you gonna tell me what had you hightailing it out of Bluestone so quickly?"

Right. He'd left quite a lot of information out during his short phone call to beg for vacation days. "My friend, he was hurt. Badly. And I needed to be there for him."

The sheriff took his time contemplating Brady's answer before replying. "How's your friend now?"

"Not in the best shape, but he'll make it."

"And you ... how are you doing, Brady?" Clarkson's usual gruff tone took on a gentler edge. concern flickering in his grey eyes.

Brady scrubbed his hands across his jaw. *Damn, I need to shave, I must look like shit.* "I'm doing better, sir. Actually, that's in large part thanks to you."

Clarkson cocked his head. "Oh really?"

"You were right. I wasn't taking my rehab seriously. And if you hadn't kicked me in the ass and forced me to go back to PT, then I'm honestly not sure where I'd be right now."

A rare smile quirked up his boss's lips. "Nice to know the threat of desk duty works on you, Deputy."

"I appreciate you stepping in, sir, really, I can't thank you enough."

"Anytime, Brady, anytime." Clarkson's smile widened. "Take the weekend off. Your shifts are covered until Monday. Go see your girl."

Will she want to see me is the real question?

"Appreciate that, sir."

That went much better than he'd expected. Not one to look a gift horse in the mouth, he took his extra days off and ran before his boss had a chance to change his mind.

***

Brady had a big romantic gesture all planned out. Well, in his head it was planned out at least. So when Alice started banging down his door, he was frozen for a moment, unsure of what to do. For a second he considered pretending he was out, but that would be madness. She was all he'd thought about for seven days. The idea of her being only yards away had his whole body convulsing.

Trying to calm his nerves, he took a few deep breaths as he strode toward the front door. He needed to remember what he wanted to say, but as he opened the door, his mind unhelpfully went blank. All air left his lungs as he looked into Alice's deep blue eyes.

Jesus, she's beautiful.

They both stared into each other, neither of them saying a word. His heart was hammering against his chest. This was his chance, and he had to take it.

Get your shit together and start fighting.

"Ali." His attempt to speak came to a sudden halt as she said his name at the same time.

They both laughed nervously, yet it did nothing to dissipate the newly thickened air.

"Please, let me go first." There was a hint of trepidation in her voice. He wasn't sure if he was going to like what she had to say, but he nodded in agreement for her to continue anyway.

"Um, okay … I had this speech in my head, but it's all a bit fuzzy now, so you'll have to bear with me."

"Speech?" His lips twitched. She was cute when she was flustered.

"Yeah, um, okay. So …" she sputtered as she straightened her spine, a look of defiance plastered across her delicate features. "When I first met you, I wanted to throat-punch you and I wasn't sure why. It was such an extreme reaction, especially for me."

"Sweetness," he warned, "I'm not sure I'm gonna like this speech of yours." Even with the very real possibility he was about to have his heart ripped out, he could feel a smile forming.

"Brady Mitchell, will you shut the fuck up for one second, please? See, this is what I was talking about. You bring out something in me that no one else ever has. I guess for the first few weeks I knew you, it was mostly a lot of violent thoughts. But after that kiss ..." She let out a sigh. "After that kiss, you brought out something else. You made me want you. Want you in a way I've never wanted anyone else, ever before. And you know what? That scared the shit out of me."

"Sweetness." He took a step forward, no longer able to keep his distance. She looked so vulnerable, he just wanted to wrap her up in his arms and promise that everything was going to be all right.

She lifted her palm to stop him from coming any closer. "Just let me get this out, okay?" she pleaded.

Going against all his instincts to touch her, he bit down on his lower lip and nodded.

"I thought that I could do the whole friends-with-benefits thing. I thought that by letting myself have that, it was enough, that it would satisfy any cravings we both had but at the same time I'd be protecting myself from pain." She let out a humourless laugh. "I'm an idiot, I know. You knew from the start it was more. You kept trying to tell me, but I didn't listen, and then I was at your door and ... and ... that woman. When she opened your door, Brady, ..." Her voice was trembling.

He just couldn't take it anymore. Giving in and wrapping his arms around her, he pulled her into his chest. His lips hovered over her ear. "Sweetness, no woman has existed for me since I first laid eyes on you. I promise you that."

Pulling back slightly, she remained in his arms but tilted her head up to look into his eyes. "I'm sorry I ran away when you told me … when you said…"

She didn't finish her sentence, instead she went up on her tiptoes and claimed his lips. The kiss was soft and slow, yet his pulse still quickened as she opened for him. She tasted of coffee and cupcakes, but the sweetness was no match for the chocolate scent he inhaled as he surrendered to the intoxication.

Breaking their connection, she remained close, a look of something he couldn't quite figure out sparkling in her eyes. "Brady, I made a decision last night … I don't want to be scared anymore. This past week, not being with you, well, it hurt more than I ever could have imagined. What I'm trying to say is that … I'm in love with you. I love you. And—"

He didn't need to hear anymore. He slammed his mouth back onto hers. She was in love with him. A mix of emotions swirled through him. He was happy, content, humbled and one lucky son of a bitch. They were done wasting any more time. Their lips still entwined, he lifted her and waited for her legs to wrap around his waist. Once she was secure, he was on the move. Kicking the front door shut with his boot, he then carried her up the stairs.

"Does this mean you forgive me?" she muttered into his mouth.

He waited until they were at the foot of the bed before he drew back and stared into those mesmerizing sapphires. "Baby, don't you get it yet? You've just made me the happiest man alive. And, sweetness, now that I know you love me, I'm never letting you go."

"Promise?"

"I promise." He tightened his grip on her behind and traced his tongue across the shell of her ear, delighting in her body's reaction. "Let me show you just how much I love you, Ali."

***

"You never told me where you've been this past week?"

Alice shifted in his arms and continued to run her fingers across his bare chest.

"We haven't exactly had time to talk, sweetness." He didn't need to look down to know she had a matching smirk. They were still in bed, and he had no plans to leave it anytime soon. As he gently stroked back her hair, he told her all about what happened with Ace.

It felt good to talk to her. If they were going to do this, then they were going to do this properly. Open and honest all the way. With that in mind, he used their talk as an opportunity to tell her about his own injury and how it had felt when he'd woken up in the hospital.

"Ever since that day, I've just felt broken. Useless. Like half a man."

"Brady—"

Cutting Alice off, he continued. "Being a marine was all I had. All I knew. I've got no living family. Had no woman. Or even a pet. I just had my team and my job. And in one day, everything I had was all taken away from me. I lost everything."

Alice was quiet for a while, when she did speak, it was whispered. "Do you still feel broken?"

"Sometimes," he admitted, "less since you came into my life. I want to fix myself for you, Ali. You deserve a man who is whole."

Alice's head snapped up as blue fury filled his vision. "You are whole! And there is not one goddamn thing you need to *fix*, Brady Mitchell—do you hear me?"

Even with the intensity of their conversation thickening the air, his woman never failed to bring a smile to his face. "Yes, ma'am."

That was the right answer and satisfied her enough to curl back into his chest. They both stayed like that for a while. Quiet. Eventually, he was the one to break the silence.

"It took me a long time to accept my new limits. But I'm getting there."

"It will get better," she reassured him as her hands

continued to caress his torso. "You've gotta know that your flexibility is a lot more advanced than most people with similar injuries. And God knows this six-pack hasn't suffered."

He let out a short laugh as she traced each ridge and muscle. "Well, that's all that matters, sweetness, keeping my woman happy."

After crawling up his body, she planted a soft kiss on his lips. "Oh, I'm more than happy."

Even though a part of him knew he may never feel good enough for Alice, looking into her eyes, he knew that he'd spend his life doing everything he could to make her happy. No one would ever love her more than he did, and that was enough. He may be a little bit broken, but Alice Hart was making him whole again.

"I love you, Brady."

A peace he never knew existed settled over him. This is what being content must feel like. "I love you too, Ali." He couldn't resist giving her another kiss before she returned her head to his chest. "You know, with you knocking down my door, I never got to give you my speech."

She looked up at him, her chin pressed into his pecks. "You had a speech? I bet it wasn't as romantic as mine." Alice grinned.

"Well, sure, it didn't start with 'when I met you I wanted to throat-punch you,' but it was pretty good."

"Okay, I'm ready. Give it to me."

He raised his eyebrow, a cheeky grin on his face as his gaze ran down the length of her body.

"Brady! That's not what I meant, and you know it."

"Okay, sweetness." He laughed as he twisted them both so they lay face to face on their sides. "When I planned on knocking *your* door down, this is what I was gonna say." He took his time running his hands down the curve of her waist while staring into her eyes. "I know you've been hurt. I know you're scared to trust me, but I'm not going anywhere. Whether it takes a week, a month, a year, *ten years*, I don't care. I'm going to show you that you can trust me with your heart. That I'll keep it safe. Always. 'Cause you're it for me, Ali. I'm never gonna stop loving you, and I'm never gonna stop fighting for you."

Unshed tears glistened in her eyes. "Damn you, Brady Mitchell."

"You didn't like it?" He couldn't help but chuckle.

Without answering, she pushed his shoulder until he was flat on his back again. She then proceeded to climb onto him until she was straddling his hips. Giving him a view he wasn't quite sure he deserved, but he was going to bask in all the same.

"I didn't have a chance, did I? You were always going to worm your way into my heart. With your silver tongue, that stupidly sexy face, and that goddamn uniform. I never stood a chance."

"Stupidly sexy face, huh?" He bucked his hips and watched her giggle as she bounced above him.

As soon as she dipped her head, he caught her lips. He was never letting go. She was his forever.

EPILOGUE

One year later

"One week," Alice beamed as she straddled his lap.

The early morning sunshine glowed behind her glossy waves, which were the only thing concealing her bare chest. Waking up to Alice never got old. Waking up naked with Alice was what he imagined heaven might feel like.

"One more week, sweetness, then you're gonna be mine. Well, legally anyway. Mrs. Alice Mitchell."

"I like the sound of that. Say it again." A sexy smirk tipped the side of her mouth as she positioned herself over him.

Tightening his grip on her waist, he held her steady as her soft lips lightly brushed his.

"Mrs. Alice Mitchell," he repeated, unable to wipe the smile off his face.

He let out a guttural groan as she ran the tip of her tongue across the seam of his lips. Parting her, he allowed her to take the lead and let her taste wash over him.

The past year had been the happiest of his life. He thought he would never be able to top the high of having Alice tell him she loved him, but the day she moved in topped it. The day she agreed to be his wife, topped it again. And in one week, when she was finally going to become Mrs. Mitchell, he had a feeling the bar would skyrocket.

Just as he was getting ready to get lost in his woman, the sound of the front doorbell rang out around them. Nothing good would come from getting out of his bed right now. Maybe whoever was out there would get bored and leave. Then the bell rang again. And again. A groan slipped from his throat as he dragged himself off Alice's soft lips.

"Booo!" she heckled as he plucked her off his lap and settled her next to him.

"I know, sweetness, trust me. No one is more upset than me." He chuckled at her pout as he exited the comfort of his bed and shucked on some sweats. "I'll get rid of them. Don't you dare put any clothes on! When I come back, I'm gonna show you all the perks that come with being Mrs. Mitchell."

"Promises, promises."

He gave her a wink before leaving. The doorbell rang again as he started down the stairs. Who on earth just showed up without calling first?

As he swung the door open, he realised just who.

"What the hell are you doing here?" Brady's mouth hung open.

"Is that any way to welcome your brother?" Ace's huge grin creased the angry burn marks on the side of his face.

Brady pulled the big man in for a hug. Ace was the last person he had expected to see. "Seriously, man, what are you doing here? I thought you couldn't make the wedding?"

Ace pulled back and rubbed the back of his neck. "Yeah, see, that's the thing. As much as I'd like to lie and tell you I'm here to see you get married man, that wouldn't strictly be the truth."

"Okay," Brady said slowly.

"I'm here to take you up on your offer. You said to look you up if I ever needed a place or a job. That offer still on the table?"

Brady couldn't believe his ears. He'd spent the past year trying to convince his friend to move to Bluestone so he could look out for him, and now here he was voluntarily. Finally.

"You don't even have to ask, man. Come on in." He stepped aside and ushered Ace into the kitchen.

His quality time with Alice wasn't going to be happening, so the least he could do was make her some coffee. After putting on a pot, he leaned against the counter, facing his friend.

"So, what changed your mind?"

Ace ran his hands through his shaggy brown hair. "There's nothing in Texas for me anymore. People I used to know feeling sorry for me, the pitying looks. I'm over it, man. I need to be somewhere else, anywhere else."

Brady studied his friend for a while, trying to formulate a plan. "You got any idea what kinda work you wanna do?"

"Not really. Something manual. I got a lotta fucking energy to burn right now."

Brady nodded in understanding. Throwing yourself into something physical was sometimes the best thing you could do. Especially for a man like Ace.

Once the coffee was brewed, he took down three mugs and started to pour. The smell must have stirred his bride-to-be as moments later she padded down the stairs in just his T-shirt. She looked sexy as hell and completely inappropriate for company.

Before he could tell her to get her ass back upstairs, though, she launched into his friend's arms.

"Ace! What are you doing here? Did you come for the wedding?"

Ace chuckled as he lifted her off the ground and swung her around. "Nice to see you too, darlin', still as beautiful as ever I see."

"All right, all right. No manhandling the Mrs., brother. Put my woman down and find your own." Brady tucked Alice into his side as soon as he got the chance, squeezed her hip, and ignored his friend's mocking laugh.

Over coffee, Brady filled Alice in on Ace's extended stay. She immediately offered up the guest bedroom and started listing all the jobs in town and at the VA Clinic that she was aware of. Brady was glad his friend was going to be close by. This past year had been rough on Ace, and even though they'd been over to Texas to visit him often enough, Brady had to admit he'd been worried.

Ace had undergone extensive treatment for his burns, each one taking a toll on him. Not only was his brother trying to readjust to a life outside of the military, but he also had to get used to his new scars. And by the looks of it, he wasn't doing so well with either.

Once they were all fully caffeinated, Brady was about to demand Alice go upstairs and put some more clothes on when the doorbell rang again.

"You've got to be kidding me," he huffed as he stood and made his way over to the door to greet yet another unexpected guest.

"Ivy!" Alice screeched from behind him. "I totally forgot you were coming by. I'm not dressed yet. Let me quickly go up and change. I'll be right back!"

Now she wants to change.

He let out a snigger as he heard her rushed footsteps clambering up the stairs behind him. "Come on in, Ivy."

Ace's eyes were all over Ivy as soon as they came through the door. Shy, sweet country girls weren't usually his friend's kind of thing. Although, thinking about it, Brady wasn't completely sure what kind of woman Ace was interested in. In all the years Brady had known Ace, he'd never exactly been Mr. Commitment.

"Ivy, this is my friend Ace. We served together. Ace, this is Ivy. She runs the Moonrock ranch a few miles down the road."

Brady noticed Ivy's cheeks pinken as she offered his friend a timid smile. *Interesting.*

"Pleasure." His friend smirked and continued to let his

eyes rove over her.

On the verge of shooting his brother a look to cut it out, a thought occurred to Brady. "Actually, Ivy, Ace, here, is looking for a place to stay. You still got those ranch-hand cabins at Moonrock?"

She suddenly looked sheepish. "Actually, I do. I had to let most of the ranch hands go a few months ago. The ranch is, um … it's having a few issues."

"You're running a whole ranch by yourself?" Ace asked, concern clearly lacing his tone.

"Um … yeah. I guess. It's no big deal." Her pink cheeks shifted to scarlet.

"Like hell it isn't. How about I help you out in exchange for staying in one of those cabins you mentioned?" Ace straightened, placing his thumbs in his belt loops.

Ivy bit down on her lower lip, clearly unsure. Brady didn't quite know what to make of the offer himself if he was being honest. His friend didn't normally go around offering his services to damsels in distress.

"Um … I don't know. I mean, you're welcome to stay in one of the cabins for as long as you want, but there's no need for you to help out. I couldn't ask you to do that."

Ace stalked over to Ivy, a sparkle in his eyes, one that Brady hadn't seen for quite some time. "Trust me, sugar, you'd be doing me a favour."

Brady watched on, suddenly wishing he had some popcorn. This was definitely going to be interesting. As Ivy and Ace's gazes remained intertwined, Alice appeared beside him.

"What did I miss?"

ISOBEL REED

SEE WHERE THE BLUESTONE SERIES BEGAN:
Love Tools

What happens when the king of casual meets the queen of picking the wrong men?

Lily is running. From a dead-end job, a neurotic mother and all the losers she dared to date. Moving halfway across the world to Bluestone County seemed like a good idea at the time. So did reopening her estranged father's hardware store. But now she isn't so sure.

Small town living has its perks though. Wide-open space, clean air, and sexy cowboys. Well, one sexy cowboy. Jake. Who also just so happens to be the new bane of her existence. At least when he's not talking, she can admire the view.

Jake is the king of casual. The love of his life has always been his ranch, and that was fine with him. He never really saw the point in long-term. But all that changes when a mouthy, blonde sasses him into oblivion. He should have known she'd be trouble as soon as he laid eyes on her. Now it's too late. She's all he can think about. All he has to do is convince her that he's finally the right man.

Isobel Reed's hilarious, emotionally charged romance will have you holding your side with laughter or reaching for a tissue. Reminiscent of small-town romance by Tessa Bailey or Kristen Ashley, you will fall in love with LOVE TOOLS and Isobel Reed's unique writing style.

EXCERPT

Lily took the opportunity to scan his face and let her eyes wander down him. His broad shoulders filled out his check shirt that pulled tight across his muscled chest. She tried her hardest not to gawk as her gaze travelled down farther to his mud-stained denim jeans that moulded perfectly to tensed thighs.

Holy shit, he's hot. Do all the men in Montana look like this?

"You about done checking me out, darlin', or do you want me to turn around and show you the back?"

She felt her cheeks flame as her eyes flicked back up and she caught sight of his cocky grin. Before she could attempt to deny what she'd been doing, his expression turned more serious as he gave her a once-over. "I didn't know Matt had a daughter."

Surprise, surprise.

"No shit. He wasn't exactly father of the year."

Lily couldn't help but think of the irony. Her father had become friends with some guy young enough to be his son, yet he still couldn't quite be bothered to pick up the phone and call his own daughter.

Marlboro Man's smile became crooked as his glare intensified. "You always swear like a trucker, darlin'? Here I thought English women were all class and manners."

Is he being fucking serious?

She let out a huff; she couldn't believe the nerve of this guy. "I'm sorry, have I stepped into the past? Are you gonna ask me why a little woman like me isn't married next?"

"All right, sweetheart, calm down." He sniggered, clearly amused by the steam coming out of her ears.

NOW AVAILABLE IN EBOOK AND PRINT
WHERE BOOKS ARE SOLD

DON'T MISS THE THIRD BOOK IN THE BLUESTONE SERIES:
Hero Complex

Chapter One

The sun wasn't even up yet, and Ivy was already having an existential crisis. Even the warm, orange glow from the table lamp did nothing to flatter the reflection staring back at her. At this point, she didn't even know how long she'd been looking at herself. It wasn't like anything was going to change just because she willed it.

Internally she berated herself. She didn't have time for this. She had chores to do. Horses to feed. And a sexy as hell man to try not to humiliate herself in front of.

"Fucking YouTube." She huffed under her breath before dragging herself away from the tilt of her floor length mirror.

Damn you Pricilla28! I'm not feeling sexy OR confident. What a load of crap.

She didn't have time to wallow in the YouTube star's betrayal. Or dwell on her poor judgment at trying out a new hair tutorial at stupid o' clock in the morning. Right now, she really did have things to do. And that meant leaving the confines of her bedroom with her new hairstyle, which was much more male Viking warrior than the sexy, feminine goddess look she was going for.

Damnit all to hell.

Letting out a heavy sigh, she dragged herself and her manly braid downstairs in search of caffeine. Caffeine wouldn't disappoint her at least. Caffeine was consistent. Reliable. Not at all filled with lies.

Coffee brewed, she was just one sip away from bliss when a loud knock had her cursing again. Back was that funny feeling in her stomach. She knew exactly who was at the door. It had been the same person for the past five days now. Ace. Sweet, kind, thoughtful Ace. And quite possibly the most beautiful man she'd ever seen.

Stop swooning and get it together.

After attempting to plaster on her most neutral, non-swoony facial expression, she made her way through the living room and down the familiar dark green hallway. A frown cracked her mask as she took in her surroundings. All this time she'd been worrying about the state of herself instead of the state of the house. What must he think? The house was in just as bad shape as everything else in her life.

Ignoring the shockingly loud creak, she flung the front door open and was treated to the best view in town. Her eyes darted to that perfectly chiselled chest first. Thank the lord for her laundry skills because if she didn't know any better, she was the reason his shirt was currently straining to contain his pecks. And she just couldn't bring herself to be sad about it. Or guilty. She'd done womankind a service if anything.

When her gaze finally drifted up to the dark stubble dotting over his square jaw, it was his intense blue eyes that captured her. She was drowning in them. So much so, it wasn't until Ace cleared his throat that she snapped out of the spell he had her under.

"Mornin' darlin'." There was that deep, smooth

southern drawl that never failed to set butterflies swarming in her stomach. "Can I come in?"

That's about the time she realised she still hadn't said anything.

"Of course. Sorry, sorry. I'm still half asleep. Come in, come in. I've got coffee, well I just made some. Just this minute. So, you're right on time." Her enthusiasm was verging on manic, but she'd just been caught gawking and desperately needed to distract him from the heat she knew was now darkening her cheeks.

The word vomit continued as she led him past the duct tape covered couch, "Did you sleep well? I mean, is the cabin okay? It's getting colder now, I'm not sure how warm it's going to be out there this winter. Maybe I could get you some extra blankets. Do you need extra blankets? I'm sure I have some upstairs. Maybe I should go –"

Before she could finish, strong arms spun her around and gripped her biceps. Ace was in her space. His head was dipped, and his mouth was just a breath away from her. How was she supposed to form coherent sentences now? And that smell. Sweet baby Jesus. He smelt like sandalwood and sunshine.

"Darlin' you need to take a breath. What's going on with you today? And what the hell happened to your hair?"

If her cheeks weren't red before, they were definitely flaming now. Quickly scrambling out of his hold she fumbled with her braid, clumsily untying it until a mass of messy brown hair hung over her shoulders.

"I was trying something new, that's all. It was much harder than it looked online, if you must know. I'm sorry you're so offended by it!"

He closed the distance between them, his large finger skimmed her chin until he'd tilted it upwards. That was when she once again found herself staring into those deep blue pools. "Sugar, it's not you, that's all. I wasn't tryin' to be rude. You're finer than a frogs' hair split four ways. You don't need nothin' doing to that pretty little head of yours."

What the hell does that mean? A frog's hair… does an amphibian comparison count as a compliment?

It was bad enough she looked a mess. Now, she felt like one too. Taking a step back, she attempted a smile. He'd rattled her. He was always rattling her. With his weird compliments and intense, longer than socially acceptable, eye contact. Great. Now her palms were sweating. She'd officially hit her humiliation limit for the day, and it wasn't even five thirty yet. Coffee. She needed coffee.

Turning her back on the big, beautiful man before her, she scurried over to the kitchen. She heard him follow behind but decided to avoid looking at him at all costs, for fear she'd say something stupid or get even redder. After pouring a mug of the muddy liquid for him, she expertly handed it over without meeting his gaze. She was doing so well. Until she wasn't. Apparently, grazing his hand was too much for her hormones. Her hand instinctively jerked at the feel of his touch.

Perfect. He thinks I'm a freak. A jumpy, babbling, sweaty, red freak with bad hair. Is it time for the earth to swallow me whole yet?

COMING SOON!

ABOUT THE AUTHOR

Isobel was born and raised in London. She still lives along the River Thames with her husband and her substantial book collection. Ever the hopeless romantic, she fell in love with the genre from a young age and was inspired to write her own stories. When she's not feasting on romantic comedies or binge reading her hoard of contemporary romance novels, Isobel is writing.

https://www.facebook.com/isobelreedbooks
https://www.instagram.com/isobelreedbooks/
https://www.isobelreed.net/
https://www.amazon.com/author/isobelreed
https://www.goodreads.com/Isobel_Reed
https://www.bookbub.com/authors/isobel-reed